KU-498-533

LINDA MITCHELMORE

HOPE FOR HANNAH

Complete and Unabridged

LINFORD
Leicester

First published in Great Britain in 2013 by
Choc Lit Limited
Surrey

First Linford Edition
published 2018
by arrangement with
Choc Lit Limited
Surrey

Copyright © 2013 by Linda Mitchelmore
All rights reserved

A catalogue record for this book is available
from the British Library.

ISBN 978–1–4448–3716–2

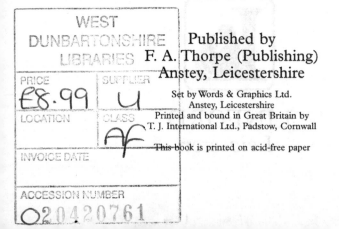

WEST
DUNBARTONSHIRE
LIBRARIES

PRICE
£8.99

SUPPLIER
U

LOCATION

CLASS
AF

INVOICE DATE

ACCESSION NUMBER
020420761

Published by
F. A. Thorpe (Publishing)
Anstey, Leicestershire

Set by Words & Graphics Ltd.
Anstey, Leicestershire
Printed and bound in Great Britain by
T. J. International Ltd., Padstow, Cornwall

This book is printed on acid-free paper

1

Spring 1903

'Hannah French, where do you think you're going?'

'Oh, Ma. Queen Victoria's been dead two years now — times are changing. I don't need a chaperone to walk a few hundred yards from the house.'

Hannah sighed. Where did her mother think she was going up here on the moor, for goodness sake? Where *was* there to go, apart from across the bracken and the heather into ever more moorland? Sometimes she felt so trapped. There was another world out there beyond the moors and Hannah longed to see it.

'And more's the pity. I hope you're not meeting someone, my girl.'

Hannah's widowed mother, Edith, tipped flour from the scale into a bowl then threw in a generous pinch of salt.

1

She turned her back on Hannah to fetch butter from the meat safe beside the back door. And Hannah knew that turning her back was her mother's way of saying the conversation was closed.

But Hannah needed to let her mother know that she was nineteen years old now, a young woman with a job at the village school, and that she couldn't be treated like a child any more.

'Who is there to meet?' Hannah said. 'There's only cows and sheep out there.'

'And rough farmhands with too much beer in their bellies.'

'Not everyone's like Pa was.'

Hannah heard her mother's sharp intake of breath. Hannah's father had worked in the tin mine at Birch Tor and just mentioning him was often enough to get her mother flying into a rage. He'd drowned in the West Dart after a day drinking at just about every alehouse within a five mile radius.

'And thank the good Lord for that,'

Edith said, taking a knife and chopping the knob of butter angrily in half, adding it to the bowl to make pastry.

Hannah bit her lip — her memories of her pa coming home drunk and picking a fight with her ma were all too raw still. Hannah had lain on the lumpen mattress of her cot up in the attic, her fingers in her ears to muffle the sound of their shouting.

'I won't be meeting any farmhands, Ma,' Hannah said. She picked up her book. 'I don't suppose many would share my love of poetry.'

'Poetry? What good's that going to be to you? Knowing 'ow to judge just when the cream's ready to clot would be far more useful to you . . .'

'I want better for myself than making cream, Ma,' Hannah said.

'You do, do you? Well, let me tell you, we'd be down the workhouse if I didn't lower myself to go and work for Sarah and Matthew Hannaford every day. And avoid Matthew Hannaford's groping paws.'

Hannah knew all about Matthew Hannaford's groping paws — she worked at Dewerbank on Saturdays and Sundays herself — and the way he came into the daily and brushed as close to Hannah as he dared when there were other girls in there, almost challenging her to say something, but knowing she never would. And if she was alone, well, then she'd feel the hardness of him against her thigh and the thought of it made her retch. Dirty old rat.

Hannah much preferred working at the village school even if it meant that, as well as listening to the children read and helping them with their numbers, she also had to clean out the privies and clear up after the little ones who had accidents in their drawers.

'I'll bring you a sprig of gorse, shall I?' Hannah said, changing the subject.

There was always gorse in bloom throughout the year somewhere on the moor, and its honey scent filled a room better than any florists' flowers could.

'Just so long as you remember what I said about farmhands. And quarrymen, for that matter. They'm's worse — a whole lot worse. More money, see, for beer. And spirits.'

'No quarrymen either,' Hannah said. 'Now, can I go?'

But Hannah didn't wait for an answer. She fled out the back door, ran across the grass and clambered over the low dry-stone wall that marked the boundary between their rented cottage and the open moor. She was free. For an hour or so, anyway.

'*How do I love thee? Let me
    count the ways,*
*I love thee to the depth and
    breadth and height*
My soul can reach, when . . .'

Hannah halted in her reading and closed her eyes, her heart full with the beauty of the poem's words.

'Don't stop,' a voice said. A man's voice.

Hannah's heart leapt with the shock of hearing it. She'd been so wrapped up in her reading that she hadn't noticed anyone approaching, although she was used to ramblers — and sometimes a photographer or an artist — walking by and passing the time of day.

'Elizabeth Barrett Browning,' she said. Had she really said that? This man was making her feel flustered and the name of the poet she was reading had just rushed out unbidden.

*   *   *

She shot a sly glance back towards the speaker and saw that he was astride a sleek, chocolate-brown horse, a very worn saddlebag hanging low on one side. He had crow-black hair; thick and worn longer than she'd ever seen on a man in these parts. She thought she might have seen him in the church at Princetown the Christmas just gone, but couldn't be certain.

'Good day to you, Miss Browning,' the man said.

'*I'm* not called Miss Browning!' she laughed. 'Elizabeth Barrett Browning is the poet who wrote what I was reading.'

'Ah,' he said.

Obviously he was no poet, no reader of literature. But he wasn't a rough quarryman either. Or a farmhand. His horse had thoroughbred written all over it, from the tips of its ears to its shiny hooves; it was well cared for and this man probably had servants to do the caring.

He seemed reluctant to ride on, so Hannah said, 'I'm Hannah French. I live over there.' She waved an arm in the direction of Hillside Cottage. A plume of smoke rose straight up into the sky in the still air.

'Pleased to meet you, Miss French. William Lawlor from Huckstone House, and latterly Furzevale Quarry.'

He leaned down and held out a hand and Hannah scrambled to her feet to shake it.

'And I you,' Hannah said, her hand still in his. 'Have I seen you before? In St Michael's at Christmas perhaps?'

Like the rest of the village and hamlets around, Hannah and her mother were regular churchgoers. Every time Hannah entered the church, she shivered to think it had been built by American and French prisoners of war, though. And always, as she walked through the graveyard afterwards, she averted her eyes from the simple tablets erected for late inmates of the prison — convicts — that gave just their initials and a date of death. How horrid it must be to be locked up in Dartmoor Prison, whatever the reasons for being there.

'I was there with my uncle, yes. The snow prevented the carriage going down into Tavistock, to St. Eustachius. My uncle prefers we all worship there. Although, I have to say, I don't worship as often as I should. Too many pulls on my time.'

His smile widened as though he was

rather glad not to go to church too often. Hannah wondered what those pulls might be — work at his uncle's quarry? A wife and family? Still he didn't let go of her hand. Would it be rude to pull it away?

Hannah wriggled her hand in his just a little bit.

'My apologies,' he said, finally letting go. 'I was looking at the view.'

He dismounted and, in one swift movement, pulled the saddlebag from his horse and opened it.

'I really must capture this view,' he said. He paused, his eyes on Hannah's and yet not really looking into them — as though his mind was somewhere else or he'd forgotten what it was he was about to say. Then he seemed to remember and said, 'Not that it's as pretty as you.'

Hannah shivered. She'd been warned about men who knew how to get women to lie with them for a few sweet words — her own mother served as a good example, and not so long ago either.

'Well, the view isn't going away,' Hannah said. 'It's been here for hundreds of thousands of years. You can come back any time. I was reading. In solitude.'

'Ah,' William said. 'Then my apologies. I won't intrude.'

He made to leave, but in his haste brushes and tubes of paint and a pad of paper fell from his bag onto the path. Hannah rushed to pick them up.

'Are you an artist?' she asked.

'I like to think I will be one day. I mean, paint for money and not just for pleasure.'

'Can I look? At your paintings?' Hannah began to straighten the sheets of paper she'd picked up.

'You most certainly can,' William said.

He held out his hands for Hannah to return the paintings and then sat down on a rock. A rock just big enough for two to sit on. There were other rocks strewn about but none near enough that she would be able to see William's paintings easily as he held them up for her. To sit beside him or not?

'I'm sorry I can't offer you anywhere more comfortable to sit, Miss French,' William said. He gestured for Hannah to sit on the flat-topped rock. Then he knelt beside her in the grass.

'This is Tavy Cleave,' William said. 'Do you know it?' He smiled at Hannah in a way that made her heart lose its steady rhythm, just for a beat or two.

Was this what it felt like to be falling in love? Hannah wondered. Then she chided herself for being so silly — it was the poem she'd been reading that was making her feel this way, wasn't it? And besides, a man whose uncle owned a house the size of Huckstone House, and who was going to inherit Furzevale Quarry one day, was hardly likely to fall in love with Hannah, daughter of the widowed Edith who lived in a tiny — and damp, most of the time — cottage.

'It's very good,' Hannah said. 'But I

don't know Tavy Cleave.'

William's painting was really beautiful. Somehow he'd managed to capture the light so that it almost beamed out from the paper as it peeped around clouds. And the heather — not yet in flower here at this time of year — had also been captured to perfection, like pale amethyst. Hannah always thought it that particular shade.

'But it's not far,' William said, looking puzzled.

'It is if you have to walk!' Hannah told him.

'I'm sorry. I've offended you,' William said. 'I'll be on my way.'

'No!' she said. 'Don't go. I'm not used to talking to young men such as yourself. I'm sorry, too. For being so sharp. It's not my way usually.'

'I'm glad to hear it,' William said.

He handed Hannah another painting — just a sketch really, but of a bird with a snail in its beak.

'It's so real,' Hannah said. 'It's like poetry, only in paint.'

'Very prettily put,' William said, 'but I'm not sure it's deserved praise. I have much to learn yet.'

And then, as though Hannah wasn't sitting next to him, he took a fresh sheet of paper and a pencil and began to sketch. He didn't talk as he worked, although he hummed a snatch of some tune Hannah didn't recognise as the pencil flew over the paper.

Hannah was mesmerised as the scene in front of her was transferred to the page — every little rock, the tor in the distance, the lone rowan tree halfway down the hill, a few red berries still left on it, even though the beginnings of blossoms had started to dot the branches with their soft whiteness. The silence between them was broken only by the high peep-peep of a skylark now and then. Or the scuffling of something through the bracken — a mouse or a rabbit, no doubt.

Hannah had ceased to be alarmed by William's close presence, so she opened her book and resumed her reading.

'I can't believe I've stayed away from the moor so long,' William said, dragging Hannah back to reality, away from the beautiful words of Elizabeth Barrett Browning.

'So why *did* you stay away?' she asked.

'It's a long story. I'll give you the short version. I've only ever been here in the holidays. My uncle put me in boarding school and then through university. From there, I went to London. To study accountancy. My uncle thought it would be a good idea. You know all about my uncle, I take it?'

'I know of Mr Lawlor,' she said. 'But did you want to do accountancy? I like numbers well enough myself but I don't think I would want to be adding up and taking away and multiplying all day long.'

William laughed.

'Neither do I very much.'

'So why did you?'

'You ask an awful lot of questions, young lady.'

'I'm not that young!' Hannah said. She snapped her book shut and sat up tall. 'I'm old enough to be employed at the village school, although I'm not qualified to teach. I listen to the little ones reading. And on Saturdays and Sundays I work at the dairy up at Dewerbank.'

'And no day off?' William sounded horrified at the thought. 'Even my uncle's quarrymen get a day off.'

'Yes, and don't they make the most of it! Getting drunk at The Plume of Feathers. And every other inn between here and Tavistock.'

'That's as may be, but you should be getting a day off every week.'

'I get the morning off on a Saturday to go to the market in Princetown and on Sundays I go to church and don't have to be at the dairy until after our midday meal. Added together, that makes a day,' Hannah told him.

'Well, if you're happy with that, Miss French . . . '

'I am. Thank you.'

Her gaze met William's and for a few seconds their eyes held one another's. How beautiful his eyes were, Hannah thought — almost as dark as peat, but with little flecks of chestnut in them too.

'Would you consider . . . ?' William began, but was interrupted by a thundering of hooves coming along the track towards them. 'You idiot!' he yelled at the rider. 'That horse could catch a hoof and snap a fetlock the rate you're riding it!'

The rider reined in and, with a skitter of hooves on loose stones, horse and rider stopped.

Ralph Lawlor. Hannah had seen him at a distance many times but never this close. His likeness to William was startling close up — they could almost be twins — yet he seemed sharper somehow, his body leaner. Harder.

'Well, well, brother dear,' Ralph said. 'This is a cosy scene. And who may this be?'

He looked straight at Hannah as he

spoke, but his eyes didn't stay resting on hers. Hannah shivered as he looked at her from the top of her head to the tip of her toes. Self-conscious now of her worn shoes and the rip in her blouse which she'd not made a very good job of darning — somehow it hadn't mattered when William was looking at her — she pulled her shawl around her, crossing her arms across her bosom.

'This is Miss Hannah French, Ralph.' He touched Hannah very gently on the shoulder as he spoke. 'And this, Miss French, is my brother, Ralph.'

'Then I am *very* pleased to make your acquaintance, Miss French.'

He placed his tongue between his lips and slid it from one side of his mouth to the other as he spoke, as though he was eating some delicious morsel. The gesture made Hannah shiver once again.

'Ralph . . . ' William began.

But Ralph held up a hand to stop him.

'Cradle-snatching, that's what you're doing, Will,' he said. 'The delightful Miss French will be far better off talking with someone nearer her own age. Won't you, Miss French?'

Ralph turned to Hannah with a dazzling smile; it thrilled and terrified her in equal measure.

'I'll be the judge of who I speak to or not,' she told him. 'And now, if you will both excuse me, I have to get home for supper.'

* * *

William was aching to get back out onto the moor in the hope of seeing Hannah French. She'd come to him in dreams every night since they'd met. But always there were invoices to be made out and written up, and calculations to be done for his uncle. Ralph, obviously, hadn't had the slightest inclination to do the task while William had been away, even though their uncle's eyesight was failing and he was unable to do it himself.

'Will!'

William heard his brother calling him, but chose to ignore the call. With luck, he'd give up and go away.

'Ah, there you are,' Ralph said, flinging back the door of the study. 'Still at it?'

'No-one else seems to have bothered to do it,' William said.

He bent his head over the accounts book.

'Miss Hannah French?' Ralph said. 'Can't get her out of my mind. I don't suppose she told you where she lives, did she? You know, when you were both so cosy, side by side, up there on the moor?'

'No.'

It wasn't a lie — Hannah had only waved an arm in a general way.

'Or where she works? If she does work, that is?'

'No,' William said — a lie this time.

'Oh, I think you do,' Ralph said. 'I don't believe even you, married as you are to your drawing and your painting, are blind to the charms of Miss Hannah French.'

'And *if* I'm not, I certainly wouldn't tell you! You're reckless and heartless where women are concerned.'

Ralph guffawed with laughter.

'No matter,' Ralph said. 'I usually get what I want. I'll find her.'

2

'Miss French,' little Robbie Stratton said, his mouth and cheeks streaked with the jam sandwich he was eating for lunch, 'there's a man on a big 'orse at the gate asking for yer.'

'There is?'

Hannah hoped with all her heart it wasn't someone from the police station to say a prisoner had escaped — if it was, then the children would have to be kept in the school until it was safe for them to return to their homes. Usually a gun would be fired, followed by the frantic ringing of a bell to signal an escape, but it wasn't unknown for prisoners to escape and be gone long before their absence was noticed.

'Didn't I just say, Miss?' The small boy licked his fingers and stood studying Hannah as though waiting for a pat on the back for bringing the message.

'Is it a constable?'

'No, Miss. And 'e were asking for you, Miss.'

From where she was standing, Hannah couldn't see the gate. She looked around anxiously to see if the headmistress, Miss Pollyblank, was anywhere about. It was a cardinal sin to have personal matters intrude into school time — whoever it might be who was waiting to speak to her. When Pa had drowned, the vicar had called with the pony and trap to take her home to Ma, but even then Miss Pollyblank wouldn't let her go before the end of school at four o'clock.

'What colour horse, Robbie?' she asked.

Could it be William Lawlor asking for her? Surely not . . .

'Black. A stallion. And bigger 'n the 'orse from Tavistock what brings the meat round on Fridays.' The child's eyes went round with the thrill of the size of the horse.

Ralph Lawlor. He was the only person she knew of who had a black horse. What was he doing here?

'Can you take the man on the horse a message from me, Robbie? And you can be blackboard monitor all next week.'

'Yes, Miss!' Robbie jumped up and down excitedly on the spot. 'What do 'ee want me to say then, Miss?'

'Can you tell the man on the horse I can't talk now? Nor at all, for that matter. Can you repeat that back to me?'

Robbie did as he was told.

'Good boy.'

Then Hannah turned on her heel and began walking back purposefully towards the classrooms. If Ralph Lawlor thought she could just stop what she was doing to speak to him, then he had another thing coming.

Suddenly, there was a commotion and the children started running towards the gate. The distinct sound of horses' hooves on gravel had Hannah

spinning round towards the distur-
bance.

Running faster than she'd ever run in
her life before, Hannah reached Ralph,
who was smiling down at her from the
saddle.

'You can't come in here,' she said.

'It seems I already have,' Ralph said.

'Well, you can just turn your horse
around and go back out again.' Hannah
turned to Robbie Stratton and said,
'Close the gate after Mr Lawlor, will
you please, Robbie?'

'Yes, Miss!' Robbie said.

'I'm going nowhere.' Ralph leaned
down from the saddle until his head
was level with Hannah's. He lowered
his voice and whispered, 'Until you
agree to join me for dinner. I have the
ideal place in mind.'

Hannah felt her colours rise. How
dare he! Just who did he think he
was?

Ralph's horse reared then and he
narrowed his eyes, his forehead creas-
ing. It skittered round, kicking out with

its back legs. He flicked the side of his mount's neck with his crop, and Hannah wondered — just for a moment — if the animal might have had a harder restraint than that had she not been there.

'Can't you control your horse?' Hannah shouted at him. 'It's frightening the children.'

'With the number of ponies loose on the moor,' Ralph said, the horse back under control now, 'these brats will be well used to horses, wouldn't you think?'

'They're not brats. They're good children.'

'Well, of course,' Ralph said, obviously thinking better of what he'd just said, 'if they're under your tutelage. But you haven't answered my question, Miss French? Will you join me for dinner one evening? I can't let a pretty girl like you get away.'

The children were all staring up at her now because Ralph Lawlor certainly wasn't whispering any more

— his voice was loud, cultured, commanding.

'My sister, Rose, is walking out with James Brent,' Robbie said proudly. 'I've seen 'em, over to the place where the cows go for water. They'm always 'olding 'ands.'

'That's enough, Robbie,' Hannah said, feeling the colour in her cheeks deepen. 'And don't you go putting it about that I'm walking out with anyone. Do you hear me?'

'No, Miss,' the child mumbled.

The sooner she could get Ralph Lawlor to leave the school yard, the better it would be for everyone. She turned to him. 'Thank you for your invitation. I will consider your request.'

'And where shall I come to hear your answer?'

'Miss lives at Hillside Cottage, Sir,' Robbie said. 'Opposite The Saracen's Head. On the . . . '

'Robbie, that will do!' Hannah chided him.

'Then I shall be there on Sunday.

What time will suit?'

'Two o' clock,' Hannah said, plucking a time out of the air.

Not that she would be there then. She'd be in the dairy at Dewerbank, making cream and patting up the butter ready for Monday's market down in Plymouth. And Ralph Lawlor would find that out soon enough.

*   *   *

When Hannah reached the end of the lane that led down to the river, she was surprised to see William there. She'd purposely not gone on her usual evening walk where she might have expected William — or Ralph — to come along on their way back home from the quarry. She wasn't sure if she wanted anything to do with the Lawlor brothers. Although now, seeing William, his paintbrush held between his teeth, studying what he had just painted — and totally wrapped up in what he was doing, oblivious to her presence

— she realised she was more than happy to see him. There was a warm feeling in the pit of her stomach, making her feel relaxed and not anxious as she had been for days thinking about tomorrow when Ralph would call and find her not there.

But she had to get past William in order to pick up the path that would take her home. To go back the way she had come would mean it would be dark before she got back.

'Good evening, Mr Lawlor,' Hannah said. 'Forgive me for disturbing you. I won't keep you. I'm taking a short cut home.'

'Oh!' William said, the paintbrush falling from his mouth. It landed on a clump of gorse, the red of the oil paint flecking the yellow blossoms like freshly-spilled blood. 'I didn't know you were there. I get lost in my work, you know.'

'I can see that,' Hannah laughed. 'So I won't keep you from it.'

'Well, not if you don't want to,'

William said. 'You're welcome to stay.'

Hannah thought he looked rather sad that she was rushing away so quickly.

'Just for a few minutes then,' Hannah said. 'I won't distract you by talking, Mr Lawlor, I promise.'

'Please, Miss French, call me William. It makes me think I'm back in a stuffy office in Regent Street when anyone calls me Mr.'

'Then you must call me Hannah.'

'I shall be pleased to. I'll just wipe this brush and then get on. The sky is such a perfect shade of pink at the moment, don't you think?'

'With orange and purple bits in it,' Hannah said, looking towards the setting sun. 'It looks like the wood in the range does just before it bursts into flame.'

'Do you paint, Hannah?' William asked.

'Not well. I mix the paint for the children at school and sometimes I make a passable attempt at a tree for them to copy, but I'm no artist.'

'More of a poet perhaps?' William said.

'I have begun to write a few verses,' Hannah admitted. Until now, that had been her secret, but one she'd happily blurted out to William.

'Perhaps you could read me something?'

'I've not brought anything with me today. Another time perhaps,' Hannah said, then realised what she had said — that she wanted to see him again. He'd think her forward and no mistake.

But William seemed not to have noticed her *faux pas*. He merely smiled at her and dipped his brush in a shade of paint Hannah couldn't quite put a name to. Indigo? Violet? Purple mixed with blue?

'I did wonder,' William said, 'if I might see you on the path where we met a few days ago.'

'I've not been able to get out in the evenings since,' Hannah lied. 'My mother's not too well, so I've been doing extra chores.'

'Nothing is seriously wrong with your mother, Hannah, I hope?'

'An early summer cold. She takes with the sneezings when the blossoms come and it makes her throat sore. And she gets headaches, too.'

At least that bit was true — her mother did suffer when the blossoms came.

'I'm sorry about that, but glad that it wasn't my presence there — or my brother's — that had stopped you from walking that way in the evenings.'

'Not at all,' Hannah said, quickly. Her heart rate increased alarmingly at the reference to Ralph.

'My brother tells me he called at the school,' William said.

'He did,' Hannah said, her heart plummeting. What might Ralph have told William about that? 'And did he say he rode right into the yard and his horse shied and it frightened the children?'

'He's hardly likely to mention anything like that to me, Hannah. He knows well enough that I don't think he gives his mounts enough care or consideration. He rides them too hard and too dangerously. Never, ever, get into a carriage with my brother, Hannah. He deploys the brake on the wheel far too late on steep hills.'

'I have no intention of it,' Hannah said. 'And I promised I wouldn't disturb you by talking, and here I am doing nothing but. I'll have to be going soon. The light is starting to fade — it will be all but gone in half an hour.'

'An hour at least,' William said, looking delighted about the prospect. 'I have a flask of tea, and some cake. We could share it.'

'Oh,' she said. 'I *am* distracting you, after all. You would have finished that painting if I hadn't come along.'

'Not so,' William said. 'The light's not good for painting any more.'

And with that he took a tin flask from his saddlebag and poured the tea into a cup. Then he unwrapped a huge slab of cake and broke it in two. Hannah had never seen such a big slab of cake before, except at the Squire's funeral tea where there had been three choices of cake and Hannah had secreted a second piece in the folds of her skirt because her pa had just died, too, and she and Edith were without his wages.

'You drink first,' he said, holding out the cup towards Hannah.

It was far too sweet for her tastes, but the fact that William was sharing it with her meant it didn't matter very much.

'Mmm,' she said, 'this cake is delicious.'

'Then I shall always have a slice in my saddlebag in case I come across you walking on the moor.'

He broke off another morsel of cake and held it out towards Hannah's lips. There wasn't enough space for her to take it between her fingers so she opened her mouth and William placed it on her tongue. But, as he took his hand away again, the backs of his fingers brushed Hannah's cheek. She loved the way it felt.

When Hannah finished the cake, William began packing away his painting things.

'My horse is tied up down by the stream. We'll walk that way together, shall we?'

'I'd like that,' Hannah said.

* * *

'Are you going down with something?' her mother asked, as Hannah whisked off her shawl and laid it over the back of a kitchen chair.

She'd been putting her shawl on and taking it off again for the best part of half an hour. If they hung about much longer Ralph Lawlor would be here and she wanted them both to be far away from the cottage when he arrived. She could always claim later that she'd been called away unexpectedly — for she was sure he *would* call again.

Sunday lunch over, she was ready to go over to Dewerbank and begin the cream and butter making, but it seemed

Edith wasn't. She was dallying. She kept asking silly questions. And she kept wiping her forehead with the back of her sleeve and sighing. Hannah was beginning to feel alarmed.

'Going down with something? I don't think so, Ma,' she said, perhaps a bit over-cheerfully. 'We're going to have to go soon if we're not to be late. You know how Mrs Hannaford always tuts if we're late.'

'Let her tut,' Edith said. 'The acid-faced madam has got nothing else to do. Now I think you ought to take a powder before you go.'

Edith made to pour some water from the jug on the draining-board into a tumbler.

'Ma,' Hannah said, exasperated. 'I feel *fine*.'

'Well, you don't look fine to me. You're flushed. I hope it's not the rubella you're getting. You said it's ripped through the classroom quicker 'n a summer squall flattens corn.'

'I've had the rubella, Ma, and you

know it,' Hannah said. 'But *you* look a bit pink, perhaps it's you who's going down with something?'

'To be honest, I do keep going all hot and then cold again.'

Edith swayed for a moment then plonked herself down heavily on a kitchen chair.

'Ma?'

'It's all right. Don't fret. I've been like this a fair bit lately. Annie Leigh says it's women's things.'

'Annie Leigh's no doctor, Ma. You ought to go and see Dr Tucker.'

'What with? Doctors cost money which we haven't got.'

Hannah heard the distinct sound of hooves in the lane outside and her heart almost stopped. Trust Ralph Lawlor to be early. Anxiously, she ran to the window and peered out. But it was only Farmer Adams on his way home from the inn, as he always was this time of day on a Sunday.

'Expecting someone, Hannah?' Edith said.

'No,' Hannah said quickly. 'I thought it might have been Dr Tucker going past, that's all.'

'Pity it weren't. Perhaps if I'd offered to make him a steak and kidney pudding, he'd have looked me over for free.'

'Oh, Ma,' Hannah said. 'Let me make you a cup of tea. Mrs Hannaford can tut all she likes.'

Staff were hard to keep at Dewerbank because of Mrs Hannaford's spiteful ways. The only reason Edith stayed, and Hannah helped on Saturdays and Sundays, was because they needed the money to pay the Duchy rent.

Hannah didn't care if Ralph called now and her mother found out — she hadn't exactly done anything wrong. Only led him on that she might consider dining with him when she had no intention of doing any such thing.

Hannah made the tea. The minutes were ticking by.

'It's no good, Hannah. You'm going to have to go to Dewerbank by yourself today. One of us has to earn money. Now put that shawl back on again and keep it on and go!'

With no alternative, Hannah went.

'I like a woman with spirit, don't you?' Ralph said.

William was surprised to see him. He'd disappeared after lunch with no explanation as to where he was going or why.

William looked up briefly, then carried on writing down numbers on a sheet of paper. As far as he could tell, there were some discrepancies between the loads of stone being quarried and the amount of money they were getting for it. The men weren't liking it much that William was watching them work, counting loads in and out. Especially as they didn't usually work on Sundays. But bad weather in March had meant they were behind with orders and William was keen to make up lost time now that better April weather was here. He was paying them double money and couldn't see what they had to grumble about.

'All spirited women, or one in particular?' William asked.

'Ah, so you've been on the other end of Miss Hannah French's cunning ways.'

'I thought that was who you were meaning,' William said. He took a swig of water from a flask — it was hot and dusty in the quarry and his mouth kept drying.

'*'I'll be there at two o'clock, Mr Lawlor*', she said.' Ralph affected a high-pitched, woman's voice. 'And she fluttered her lashes at me when she said it. Except she wasn't there when I called, was she? Her mother was, though.'

Good, William thought. I'm glad Hannah saw through you. He double-checked the weight of a load of stone that had just been put into a wagon.

'Met her, have you?' Ralph asked.

'Hannah? Yes, you know I have.'

'And you know I don't mean Hannah in this instance.'

'Mrs French? No. I can't say I've had the pleasure.'

Ralph laughed.

'I thought she was going to get down and kiss my feet,' he said. ''*Oh, it's Mr Ralph from Huckstone House. What can I do for you, Sir*' she simpered at me. She's a pretty enough woman, I grant you, given her age — and it bodes well for the lovely Hannah if she isn't going to lose her looks like her ma hasn't . . . '

'Shut up, Ralph, will you?' William said. 'I need to concentrate. And, apart from that, the men don't need to hear your business.'

William flicked his head towards the quarry workers who seemed to have slowed down their efforts to listen.

And what was more, he didn't want to hear another word from Ralph. He'd heard enough.

'And if you haven't got anything better to do, you can give the men a hand. We're a worker down today — Ned Narracott's infant daughter's been taken to the Cottage Hospital.'

'Are we now?' Ralph took off his jacket and then pulled his shirt over his head. He was smiling and William thought to tell him that it was no smiling matter that an infant had been taken to hospital, but wasn't going to waste his breath. 'Cracking rocks should work off a bit of frustration, shouldn't it? Not that I was expecting the lovely Hannah to resist.'

'Harm one hair on her head . . . ' William began. But Ralph was already striding away towards the men.

3

Hannah was dragging her heels going home. Ralph would have called, she knew he would. And her mother would have spoken to him and was, no doubt, waiting to give her a piece of her mind for encouraging a man to call on her.

She took the long route back along the drovers' road. And then something caught her eye. Splashes of colour — red and blue, and green and orange in various shades — lying amongst the emerging whortleberry shrubs, like a fallen rainbow.

Tubes of oil paint. William's, without a doubt. Oil paint, Hannah knew, was expensive — not that the cost would worry someone of William's means. But losing them would mean he would have to go into Plymouth or Tavistock to get more. And he had a lot to do for his uncle — he'd told Hannah so.

Hannah picked up the tubes of paint and put them in her basket. Oh, and a small sketchpad. Hannah picked that up, too, and slowly turned the pages over. Flowers and birds and . . . oh, there was a sketch of someone; Hannah knew it just had to be her. The line of her nose, the tilt of her chin. The way her hair fell in waves and escaped any hair ornament she tried to tame it with. William had drawn her! From memory — it had to be from memory. How thrilling it felt to know that — to see that, with her own eyes.

If she hurried, she could go via the quarry. She'd heard the blasting when she'd been at Dewerbank; surprised to hear it on a Sunday. She could take the short cut that skirted the quarry to Huckstone House. William might be at home and he might not, but she'd ring the bell and give the book and oils to a servant and tell him or her where she'd found them.

But it wasn't William she saw at the quarry. It was Ralph.

He was stripped to the waist, a heavy hammer in his hand, cracking rocks as easily as if they were hazelnuts, Hannah thought. How strong he was. How muscled. How his back glistened with the sweat of his efforts. Hannah felt quite faint looking at him.

He wasn't going to be pleased to see her though, was he? Hannah wondered what sort of reception he would have had from her mother — and the other way around, no doubt. As long as Ralph stayed with his back to her, she could skirt the quarry edge then be out of sight the rest of the way to Huckstone House.

Then, as though sensing she was looking at him, Ralph turned around and looked right at her. He dropped his hammer to the ground and strode towards her. Hannah remained rooted to the spot.

He reached her in seconds, striding over piles of rock and mounds of heather; seconds when she hardly dared breathe.

'So, where were you?' Ralph said.

'At Dewerbank. I expect my mother told you as much.'

'She did.'

'Good.' Hannah took the tubes of oil paint from her basket. She was on the point of taking out the sketchbook, too, but changed her mind. Ralph might look through it and see William's sketch of her. She didn't want him to do that. 'I found these when I was walking home. I think they might be your brother's. I'll just take them to the house . . . '

'You won't,' Ralph said. '*I'll* take them.'

He held out his hands for the tubes of paint, but Hannah was reluctant to give them to him. She had an uneasy feeling that Ralph would crush the tubes of paint — make them unusable to William as a way of getting back at her for not being home when she'd said she would be.

'No. If you don't want me to go to Huckstone House, then perhaps you'll be so good as to tell your brother I have them.' She dropped the tubes of paint back in her basket. 'If he'd like to call . . . '

'And find you not there, the way I found you not there?' Ralph interrupted.

He took a step nearer and Hannah backed away, only to almost fall over a tussock of grass. She reached for Ralph to steady herself.

He grabbed her with both hands, pulled her so closely to him that Hannah could smell the residue of soap on him, mixed with sweat; the good, honest smell of a working man, her mother had always called it.

Ralph let go of her wrists and took her face gently in his hands. With a finger, he tilted her chin so she had no option but to look at him.

And then he kissed her. Hannah was unable — or unwilling? — to pull away. Against her better judgement, she found herself kissing him back. All sorts of new and wonderful feelings were flooding through her, the major one of which was danger.

'There,' Ralph said. 'Didn't you like that? I doubt my brother would kiss you so thoroughly.'

'I've yet to find out,' Hannah said, backing away from him.

She ran all the way home.

* * *

'Why didn't you tell me Mr Ralph was calling?' Edith said.

There was no point in lying to her mother, so she told the truth.

'As you see, Ma,' she said, 'he asked me at a time when I couldn't really say no. Not many days ago, you said you hoped I wasn't meeting anyone on the moor. Rough farmhands. *And* quarrymen, you said.'

'Quarrymen? Mr Ralph's heir to the quarry — a quarry owner-in-waiting, that's what he is. I've heard he does all the jobs — not just in the office, but the blasting and the loading an' all. So he'll know how the jobs should be done when the time comes for him to be the boss.'

'So I've s — ' Hannah began, then corrected herself. 'Heard.'

She thought her legs might go from under her at the memory of Ralph stripped to the waist. And his kiss. She ran a tongue over her lips — yes, she still had the taste of him on them.

'Well, I'm glad it's you he likes and not Beth Hannaford.'

'Miss Beth?' Hannah said.

Was Ralph walking out with Beth Hannaford? If he was, then he had no right kissing her — Hannah — did he?

'You'm a lot prettier than Beth Hannaford,' Edith said. 'Just think how grand it would be if you were to marry Ralph Lawlor and move up into the big house. I expect there'd be a cottage on their land I could move into. So's I'd be on hand when the little ones come along.'

'Ma, Ralph Lawlor is no more likely to ask me to marry him than you are to

48

become Queen of England. Besides, he's not the heir apparent. His older brother, William, is.'

'Shared, Hannah. It's all going to be shared. Unless one of them gets married and has a son before their uncle dies, and then it will all go in trust to the grandson.'

'How do you know all that?'

'Annie Leigh does for the Lawlors up at Huckstone House. Cleaning and that. And now Mr Charles is going blind, her 'elps out more'n 'er used to. Annie can't help hearing things.'

'It's eavesdropping.'

'That's as maybe. And that's not all she's heard.' Edith folded her arms across her waist, as though waiting for Hannah to ask what else Annie Leigh had been saying.

But Hannah merely shrugged. The last thing she wanted to hear was something she didn't want to know about — something about William.

'Seems that William Lawlor is stirring up trouble in the family. Saying that Mr

Ralph has been fiddling the books, and that half the money for those corbels for fancy bridges up to London didn't make it into the bank account.'

'Well, perhaps it didn't,' Hannah said. Nothing she could hear about Ralph Lawlor would surprise her now.

'Ha,' Edith said. 'Just because he isn't his uncle's favourite.'

'Ma, it's time you stopped believing everything Annie Leigh says is gospel.'

Edith grunted.

'Just don't go fluttering your eyelashes at William Lawlor, that's all. Because from what Annie Leigh's heard, he's not going to be much use running a quarry because he wants to go abroad and paint views.'

Abroad? William hadn't said anything about that.

★ ★ ★

'Oh,' Hannah said, as William flopped down on the grass beside her. She hastily closed her notebook — she'd been writing poetry. 'I didn't hear your horse's hooves.'

She looked around for William's chocolate-brown mare.

'That's because I'm not riding today. I wanted to get closer to the ground. Did you know, Hannah, that far from being a barren place, the moor is covered in many varieties of flower?'

Without waiting for an answer, William pulled back the grass to reveal a tiny mauve flowerhead pushing its way through the leaves.

'Oh, that's beautiful,' Hannah said, reaching out an index finger to touch the petals at the exact moment William did too. Their fingers touched and neither seemed keen to break the connection. 'What's it called?'

'I have no idea,' William laughed. 'But I mean to find out. There's a good lending library in Plymouth. Although, when I'm going to find the time to go I don't know. Would . . . would you . . . ?'

William stopped speaking and pulled his hand away to begin rummaging about in a canvas bag he had slung across one shoulder.

'Looking for these?' Hannah said. She took the tubes of oil paint she'd found from her bag.

'Oh, you found them!' William said. He looked delighted that she had.

And surprised. Hannah's guess was that Ralph hadn't told him he'd seen her on her way to Huckstone House. Or that he'd kissed her. Well, thank goodness for that!

'And this,' Hannah said, handing him his sketchpad with the drawing of her in it.

'Ah,' William said, looking somewhat embarrassed now, rather than delighted. 'I take it you've looked inside?'

'I have.'

'And?'

'You capture flowers and birds so well,' she said. 'I'm sure, when you go to Italy, or wherever it is you're going, then there will be even more beautiful things to draw there.'

'Who told you that?' William said. He

looked quite cross and Hannah was beginning to wish she hadn't mentioned it. 'My brother?'

'No, not him,' Hannah said. 'But rumours fly faster than a buzzard on a downward dive across the moor. All it takes is one person to overhear something.'

'The good Mrs Leigh?'

'I couldn't possibly say,' Hannah said, not quite catching William's eye as she spoke.

'Well, if that little snippet has reached your ears — and I have to tell you that, for the moment, I'm going nowhere — I imagine you might have heard other rumours?'

Hannah shook her head, but she wasn't at all sure it was convincingly.

William turned away from her and lay down on his stomach and began parting grass — in search of flowers to paint, Hannah assumed. He picked three, small white ones Hannah didn't know the name of, and two leaves. Then he rolled onto his back before sitting up.

'I do want to go to Italy to paint, Hannah,' William said. 'But there's too much to keep me here at the moment.'

'My ma told me,' Hannah said.

'About?'

'That you're looking into the finances of the quarry for your uncle because numbers aren't adding up . . .'

'Servants!' William interrupted.

'I'm one of those,' Hannah said, quietly.

'You're not. You work at the school.'

'And I suppose that's the only reason you seek out my company? Because I have an honourable position at a school?'

'Don't put words in my mouth, Hannah.'

'I'm not. It doesn't alter the fact, though, that I'm a servant. At weekends. For the Hannafords at Dewerbank.'

'You've already told me that. It makes no difference to me *what* you are — it's *how* a person is that matters to me. Tell me, Hannah, is there anything else about me and my reasons for being back on Dartmoor that have reached your ears?'

'I don't know that I want to say. I don't like cross words — with you, or anyone.'

'But there is something?'

'You seem to read me very well,' Hannah said. 'So, you'll know I'm lying if I say I haven't heard anything else. I've heard that your brother is walking out with Beth Hannaford.'

'News to me,' William said.

Hannah didn't know whether she was pleased or not to hear William say that. Ralph's kiss had certainly disturbed her; thrilled her. She took a deep breath to steady her thinking.

'And I've heard he does all the jobs at the quarry so he'll be better placed to know how it should run when the time comes to take over.'

'Not all,' William said.

'He was cracking stones when I saw him. I . . . '

Hannah placed her hands over her

mouth. She felt her cheeks colour and her heart rate increase rather alarmingly. Would William be able to see from the state of her that Ralph had kissed her? And that she had kissed him back?

'You went to the quarry?'

'Not intentionally. I was on my way to your house to bring back the paints and the sketchpad. But Ralph saw me. He came over to me. I was afraid he'd crush the tubes of paint, because he was cross with me about something.'

'What?'

'I'd better go. This is getting worse and worse. I was so happy to see you just now . . . ' Hannah stood up.

'Were you?' William said. 'Are you sure it's not my brother who's uppermost in your affections?'

'I'm not answering that,' Hannah said.

Because in truth, she couldn't be sure; not sure at all.

★ ★ ★

'Ah, just the man,' William said, after he'd breakfasted the next morning.

Ralph, obviously, had been up well before and out on his horse somewhere. He still had the crop in his hand and his cheeks were pink from exertion as he came striding into the breakfast room.

'The man for what?' Ralph said.

'To answer my question.'

'Which is?'

'Why didn't you tell me Hannah French was calling to return some oil paints of mine that she'd found?'

Ralph's eyes widened.

'I didn't realise I was accountable to you for my actions,' he said coolly.

'Actions?'

'Mine or the delectable Miss French's. It was just a kiss, Will, just a kiss. Although I have to say she responded most generously. Nothing more than that, though. For the moment.'

So, *that* was why Hannah had been so keen to get away after letting slip that she'd seen Ralph at the quarry.

William knew he was burning up with something . . . and that feeling was jealousy. A new feeling for him. He'd never taken so instantly to anyone before as he'd taken to Hannah. His brother would be a formidable foe if he had to fight him — metaphorically speaking — for her hand. But fight he would.

'Does Miss Hannaford — who I have it on good authority you are walking out with — know about the kiss with Hannah?'

'*Shared* kiss, Will. She kissed me back all right.'

'That doesn't answer my question. Does Miss Hannaford know?'

'I shouldn't think so. And you're not going to tell her, are you?'

Ralph slapped his crop across the palm of his hand.

The action made William shiver. He knew in an instant that Ralph wouldn't stop at hitting *him* with the crop if he felt like it.

'You're despicable.'

Ralph laughed.

'There isn't a ring on Beth Hannaford's finger yet.' He laughed even louder. 'Mine or anyone else's. So, in the meantime, what harm is there in playing the field?'

William chose not to answer the question.

'What were you doing at the quarry when Hannah came by? Breaking rocks, she said.'

'Then she told the truth. God, but you've got it bad for Hannah French. Go on, kiss her! You haven't yet, have you?'

'I don't have to answer that!'

'No, because it's all over your face that you haven't. You might be surprised if you do. I don't mind sharing. You or me first to get her into bed, Will — there's the wager.'

William stood up, knocking his chair over in his haste.

'Breaking rocks, you say? Maybe it's time I learnt other aspects of the quarry business, apart from the accounts — which, I have to tell you, are showing more than a few discrepancies.'

Ralph's colour drained from his face then.

'Come on, brother,' William said. 'What's keeping us? We'll break rocks together. Whether or not Miss Hannah French walks by.'

And with that, William made his way to the quarry. Maybe breaking rocks would dissipate some of the anger he felt towards his brother. Maybe . . .

★ ★ ★

'I can't, Miss Pollyblank. I really can't. You'll have to find someone else to go.'

Hannah was sick with fear at what Miss Pollyblank was asking her to do, and also angry at Ralph's audacity in suggesting it. Kissing him back had been a grave mistake. And yet . . . how thrilling. She'd woken in the night three times after reliving the moment in her dreams.

'I will not, Miss French. Mr Ralph has expressly asked that you accompany him to the stationers' in Tavistock, and accompany him you will. Apparently, his cousin, Daisy, will be going along, too.'

'Cousin Daisy?' Hannah said.

She hadn't heard either William or Ralph mention a cousin called Daisy living at Huckstone House. And neither had her mother passed on the possibility, via Mrs Leigh.

'As chaperone, Miss French. You don't think I'd . . . '

Miss Pollyblank rubbed her hands over and over together in her lap. Obviously the thought of why Hannah might need a chaperone to be with Ralph Lawlor had fired her imagination.

'Afternoon school is nowhere near over yet,' Hannah said.

'And I can free you from your duties if I so choose.'

But I don't choose, Hannah thought. She tried again to get out of going.

'Couldn't one of the older boys go, perhaps? David Grevitt? He'll know what things to choose.'

'No, Miss French. It has to be you. And now. Mr Ralph says he will wait for you at the crossroads rather than get the children all excited by driving a horse and carriage into the playground. He will be there . . . ' Miss Pollyblank lifted the watch pinned to her blouse to check the time,' . . . in five minutes.'

'But, my ma,' Hannah said. 'She'll wonder why I'm not home at the usual hour.'

To get to Tavistock and back, even with two horses pulling up the hills, would take ages. Hannah would be late for the evening meal.

'David Grevitt can take a note, if he's as reliable as you say. He passes Hillside Cottage. Now go and get your coat. And your hat. You can't go on a school errand without a coat and hat. And I can see Mr Ralph's carriage coming along the top road.'

'My ma likes meals to be at regular

intervals, and . . . '

'Miss French!' Miss Pollyblank said sternly.

Hannah knew all her arguments were lost. She turned towards the peg where her old black coat — too short now, but she didn't have enough money to replace it just yet — was hanging. And her hat, which she'd bought at the church jumble sale for a penny. To her, it looked like an executioner's hood.

She put both on and walked, full of dread, towards the crossroads and Ralph and his carriage.

4

'Where's your cousin, Daisy?' Hannah said. She'd allowed Ralph to help her into the carriage, fully expecting Miss Daisy Lawlor to be inside. She'd had no option but to sit because the carriage had wobbled and practically tipped her onto the leather seat. 'Miss Pollyblank said Miss Daisy was coming, too. As chaperone.'

'Relax, Hannah,' Ralph said, beaming at her. He looked, Hannah thought, like the proverbial cat that had got the proverbial cream. 'Your knuckles have gone white the way you're gripping your bag so tightly.'

Realisation hit Hannah. Ralph had tricked her, hadn't he?

'Let me out. Please,' she said, amazed at how calm she felt, how measured her words were. 'You never had any intention of asking your cousin to act as chaperone, did you? This isn't proper.'

'And neither, my dear, was that kiss you gave me.'

Hannah knew she couldn't deny that.

'You didn't come to the school to collect me because you knew Miss Pollyblank would never have let me come with you un-chaperoned. Didn't you?'

'My, but you're bright, Hannah. So maybe you'll be bright enough to see that Miss Pollyblank won't be pleased if the Lawlor charity my uncle gives her school is withdrawn? And quite possibly, if you do get out, your engagement at the school will come to an end. Miss Pollyblank won't be pleased with you one little bit if I have . . . '

'That's blackmail.'

'Incentive,' Ralph said.

'So, where is Miss Daisy?' Hannah asked.

'Not here, as you see.'

'Couldn't we go via Huckstone House and collect her?'

'We could, but she won't be there.

But, think for a moment, Hannah. Is this enough for you? A lowly position at the village school? Marriage to a farmhand, or a quarryman? I could show you a better life, a more comfortable life. Wouldn't you like that?'

'Only if it was of my choosing! Although, I have to tell you, there are farmhands and quarrymen who are gentlemen, not given to trickery.'

Ralph guffawed.

'Don't protest too much, Hannah. Let me show you a little of a different life to the one you have now, and see if you don't like it the better.'

And with that, Ralph closed the door on Hannah and leapt up into the driving seat. One shouted command to his horses, and a flick of the whip on one of them, and they were off.

★   ★   ★

'But the cost?' Hannah said, as Ralph placed yet another box on the stationers' counter.

Ralph threw his hands wide, suggesting the cost was nothing to him.

If this was showing her a different sort of life where one could spend money on others without counting the cost, then Ralph was achieving his aim. Why, already the bill had come to more than Hannah earned in six months.

'And now, my dear,' Ralph said, 'it's time we went. Mr Axworthy will have all this parcelled up and delivered to the school tomorrow. In the meantime, we have dinner waiting for us.'

'Oh, but I can't. I mustn't. My ma . . . '

'Your mother looked delighted I'd called on you. I'm sure she wouldn't object to know I am spoiling her daughter a little. You deserve spoiling, Hannah. You really do.'

And with that he placed a hand under her arm and led her from the shop.

'I'll leave the carriage here,' he said. 'A little walk will do us good.'

'Walk where?' Hannah said.

'You'll see!'

Ralph guided her along Brook Street, busy with shoppers still, and they were soon in the centre of the stannary town. As they crossed the road, Hannah looked back at the town hall — it loomed, large and Gothic, over the market square. Hannah knew it would be useless to protest without making a scene, and she didn't want that. On Ralph led her, along West Street. As they passed a milliner's shop, Hannah couldn't prevent her eyes from lingering. What wonderful hats! How much would even the cheapest be? she wondered.

'Shall we take a look?' Ralph smiled down at her. 'You're devouring those hats with your eyes, if I may say so.'

He took his hand from Hannah's elbow and reached for her hand, pulling her arm through the V of his elbow. The action startled Hannah — how intimate it was. How controlling. But again, she knew that to withdraw her arm and protest would be of no use. Ralph

68

Lawlor was obviously a man used to getting his own way.

'There'll be no point,' Hannah said. 'I wouldn't be able to afford a single one, I shouldn't think.'

'We'll simply look then, shall we?'

Ralph guided her towards the window of Perrett's. And, as Hannah had suspected, even the cheapest cost more than she earned in a week.

'They're all beautiful,' she said. 'Every single one.'

But it was a blue one, the colour of bluebells just before the buds open, that caught her eye. She couldn't look away.

And Ralph noticed.

'That one you've almost bought with your eyes will look wonderful on you,' he said.

'But it isn't going to. It's far more than I dare even think about spending on a hat. But it has given me an idea. I can trim one I have to look similar. The shop sells trimmings, I see.'

That she would have to come back to Tavistock to buy the trimmings, she didn't mention. She had a feeling Ralph would suggest bringing her if she did.

Hannah turned from the window. Yes, Ralph Lawlor was opening her eyes to finer things; she just hoped she wouldn't covet them too deeply. Because wouldn't she be breaking a Commandment if she did?

'Another time,' Ralph said, leading her on more quickly now. Hannah looked this way and that at all the wonderful shops — clothes and shoes and bags. And books. And even a shop selling violins. Her head whirled with it all.

They made a left turn down towards the river, then another left.

'We're going round in circles,' Hannah said.

Ralph laughed, guiding her across the road.

'What do you think?'

Ralph had pulled them to a stop outside The Bedford Hotel. It rose majestically, higher than the highest Dartmoor tor.

'I think it's a beautiful place, but I'm not dressed for going inside. And besides . . . '

'I promise to act as a true gentleman — not even one little kiss — if you dine with me. In fact, I think you ought, because not to have been at home when you knew I was calling was very unladylike behaviour.'

'Take me home, Mr Lawlor, please,' Hannah pleaded, aware of his nearness.

She thought about running from him but it would be a long and very steep walk home. And she had no lamp to light her way.

'Ralph. You can call me Ralph. And I *will* take you home, but not just yet. I've booked a private room for us to dine.'

At that precise moment, Hannah's stomach rumbled embarrassingly. She'd only had a hunk of bread with some cheese and a spoonful of pickle for her lunch, and that was hours ago now.

She prayed Ralph wouldn't have noticed the rumble. But then, as though her stomach were tricking her into eating with Ralph, it rumbled again. Only louder.

'I hear you're hungry!' Ralph said, smiling at her.

'I can't deny it,' Hannah said.

Ralph guided her forward and up the steps of the hotel. Within seconds, a man in a uniform of black trousers and waistcoat with a white shirt — a porter or a waiter? Hannah couldn't be sure because she'd never been in an hotel before — was showing them into a private dining room which was bigger than the entire ground floor area of Hannah's home. Beautiful drapes with tassels and fringing were drawn, shutting out the darkening sky. A table that might seat eight, never mind just the two of them, was in the centre of the room.

'Your coat, Ma'am.'

Ma'am? That was what she called Miss Pollyblank. No-one had ever called Hannah Ma'am before.

Hannah unbuttoned her coat. She

removed her hat and handed it to the man, then allowed him to help her off with her coat. So this was how those with money were treated. A little ashamed of herself for enjoying it so much, Hannah sat when a chair was pulled out for her.

Ralph waited for Hannah to sit before seating himself. There was a bottle of wine open on the table. And two glasses. The man placed one of the glasses in front of Hannah, the other in front of Ralph, and then filled them.

'The waiter will be in with your meal soon, Mr Lawlor. Ma'am.'

Ah, so he was probably a porter, Hannah decided.

The porter left.

For a fleeting moment, Hannah thought to ask Ralph how many other women he had brought here to this hotel, to this private dining room. It was obvious he was known to the staff.

But candles were flickering, casting wonderful patterns of light around the room, and it was warm. There had been delicious smells coming from the kitchen as they'd passed it. Hannah took a sip of her wine — the first she had ever had; how powerful and fragrant it tasted. She wanted to believe Ralph had no ulterior motive in bringing her here. He hadn't — after all — stopped the carriage on the way to try to kiss her, or do anything else to her for that matter, against her will. Perhaps she had misjudged him. Still, best to let him know she had no intention of showing her thanks for the meal with kisses.

'I apologise for not being at home when I knew you'd be calling. I had to go to Dewerbank . . . '

'Which you knew when you said, 'Call at two o'clock'.'

'Yes. I'm sorry.'

'Apologies accepted. Ah, here's the waiter. I've taken liberty and pre-ordered for you. I hope you don't mind?'

Hannah did. How delicious it would have been to choose; almost as good as tasting the food itself. But when the waiter placed a bowl of soup in front of her, the smell and the sight of it was enough to forgive him anything.

'It looks almost too delicious to eat,' Hannah said.

'But you must.'

'I will,' Hannah said, picking up the silver spoon beside the plate.

She knew she ought to ask Ralph if it was true that he was walking out with Beth Hannaford. And she would. Soon. But for the moment, she would drink up all these delicious, new experiences.

* * *

'You never do things by halves, Will,' Ralph said.

William halted, the chisel in his hand. Two gravestones were well overdue on delivery because the stone-mason had gone down with the influenza. After a few false starts, when stone had cracked right across when he'd hit the chisel too hard with the hammer, he was getting the idea of chasing a line, a pattern, in the granite. And he was enjoying it — another art form, as it were.

And he wasn't best pleased to be interrupted now.

He turned to face his brother.

'Meaning?'

'Meaning, getting an idea of all aspects of the quarrying is one thing, taking on the role of stonemason is another. We pay Reg Croft to do that.'

'And he's not been here for a fortnight, unless that missed your notice when you were taking the carriage and driving off goodness-knows-where, without asking Uncle Charles.'

'It's there for the taking,' Ralph said. 'Uncle Charles can't see to drive it now. And he paid off the coachman years ago when he had to close the tin mine down.'

'So, where did you go?'

'Which time in particular?' Ralph said.

'We'll start with yesterday and work backwards, shall we?' William said. 'I consider it unethical of you to claim wages and be elsewhere. And I see you claimed a full day's pay.'

'Hah!' Ralph said. 'An hour here, an hour there, to drive a beautiful lady to Tavistock. Dine with her. See the limpid pools of her eyes . . . '

'Oh, shut up! And unless you wanted me for anything particular, I'd like to get on.'

William turned the chisel around in his hand, liking the feel of the wood on his skin; warm and solid.

'Just one thing,' Ralph said. 'Should anyone ask how our cousin, Daisy, is — anyone at all — perhaps you'd be so kind as to say she's indisposed.'

'We both know we have no cousin Daisy,' William said, slowly. 'What lies . . . ?'

'Not lies, Will. Simply a bending of facts.'

William placed the chisel against the block of granite. He felt like giving it a hard clout with the hammer to expel some of the anger he felt against Ralph and his underhand ways. But all that would serve would be to split the stone.

'What shall I say *Daisy* is indisposed with? Just so our stories tally?' he asked, through gritted teeth.

'The influenza will do. Seeing as it's been hovering over the moor for weeks. And, if you'll take my advice, you'll strip to the waist in case a certain Miss French walks by. She can't resist a man with a bare chest.'

'Bugger off!' William said. He didn't want to hear any more of what Ralph might boast about, gloat about.

'Consider me gone,' Ralph laughed. 'But remember Daisy . . . '

And then the cry went up to ' Stand by' as dynamite was lit to blast more stone from the quarry face, and Ralph fled.

As the echo of the blasting died away, and the dust settled, William had a sick feeling in the pit of his stomach that he'd played the gentleman too assiduously and for too long. Ralph had captured Hannah's affections by devious means.

He ought to warn her.

* * *

Miss Pollyblank was thrilled with the purchases that Ralph Lawlor had delivered to the school. More than his uncle had ever donated to them, she'd told Hannah. 'And isn't it surprising what a pretty face and a smile can achieve?' she'd added, which had made Hannah's heart sink like a stone to around her boots. Whatever would Miss Pollyblank think if she were to know Hannah had gone alone with Ralph to Tavistock, held his arm while they walked to The Bedford Hotel? Dined with him.

But a week had passed and Hannah began to breathe a little more easily that no tales had reached Miss Pollyblank's ears. Or her mother's. She'd had to eat a second dinner that evening after Ralph had taken her to The Bedford Hotel, because to say she had already eaten would have made her mother question where, and what, and with whom. Questions Hannah wouldn't have wanted to answer.

Hannah hadn't seen Ralph since. Or heard from him. Well, she was under no illusion that she meant anything to him at all. He'd obviously achieved what he had set out to do, which was dine with her, be it with her assent or by his own cunning. But he'd shown her a different life. She could taste the roast lamb she'd eaten still. And the lemon posset pudding. It had been too delicious for words.

She hadn't seen William either — well, not to speak to. She'd seen him on his horse when she'd been cutting peat for the hearth. Thank goodness that the evenings were drawing out now so she could do tasks like that after supper. By the time she'd registered the sound of a horse's hooves on the gravelled road and looked up, all she'd been able to see had been William turning the horse before galloping back the way he'd come. She'd had to resist the urge to call after him. How forward, how unladylike that would have been, if she had.

Hannah was cutting peat again now. While the days were warm enough for late April, the evenings were cold and she and her mother still needed to huddle round the fire to keep warm.

Was William out on the moor sketching and painting? Such a big area — not that she'd seen more of it than she could easily walk in half a day.

And then, as if thinking about him had willed him to arrive, she heard the sound of a horse's hooves, getting closer; not thunderingly so, as Ralph would have ridden his horse, but with respect for his animal. She stood up. She'd make sure William saw her this time. She'd missed his quiet presence. But what a mess she must look in her oldest skirt and blouse and her most battered hat. And her boots had seen better days, too.

William brought the horse to a stop and leapt down from the saddle.

'Hannah,' he said, with a little nod.

No smile, Hannah noticed.

'William,' she said. She moved her turf-iron from her right hand to her left, readied herself to shake hands with William.

But he didn't offer his hand. Instead, he stretched a palm towards her for the turf-iron.

'Let me do that for you, Hannah,' he said. 'All week at the school, and you're still working.'

William shrugged off his jacket, threw it over the saddle of his horse.

'I'm used to it,' Hannah said.

But she handed him the turf-iron anyway.

'My brother tells me . . . ' William began, not looking at Hannah as he spoke, but he seemed to run out of words. He rammed the turf-iron hard into the earth and bits of sodden peat splattered over his boots.

Hannah guessed what it was Ralph had told him.

'That he kissed me?'

'Yes.'

'And that I kissed him back?'

'That, too,' William said. 'I realise you are at liberty to kiss whomsoever you choose. But . . . '

'I am. And I realise your brother caught me unawares. I regret that kiss now.'

Even though I enjoyed my glimpse into the world he was showing me because of it. And even though I wouldn't mind glimpsing a bit more of it, and I certainly wouldn't mind escaping the bleakness of the moor and peat-cutting and my mother's sharp tongue, she thought but didn't add.

William carried on peat-cutting. And Hannah carried on watching him. Neither of them spoke. The pile of peat turves grew higher.

'I'm getting a few calluses,' William said at last. He showed Hannah his left hand.

'Peat-cutting?'

'Not just that'

'How, then?' she asked.

'At the quarry. Stone carving. There was an order for corbels for bridges in London that got behind because the stonemason's been ill. And tombstones.'

William swapped the turf-iron over to his other hand, showing Hannah the calluses on his palm.

'They look raw,' Hannah said. 'I'm not at all sure you should be cutting peat. Your hands could become infected . . .'

'So could yours,' William said, looking serious.

He set to cutting peat again as though he'd been born to the job, Hannah thought. She helped by stacking them on her sled ready to be dragged back along the sheep track to her home. Hannah asked about the stone carving and he told her that now he was mastering the skill, he had it in mind to carve other things. Heads, perhaps. And statues.

Hannah related a funny story from school, when Tobias Short had been asked to recite the Lord's Prayer, and he'd said, 'Our Father who art in Devon, Harold be thy name.'

It was as though the incident between her and Ralph had never been, and that William hadn't mentioned it.

Hannah was grateful to William when he said he'd drag the sled back home for her. Hannah held the rein of the horse which meekly followed. William even insisted on stacking the peat up inside the garden wall, under the makeshift shelter Hannah had made for it to dry off.

Her mother must have heard voices because she came rushing out, a box in her hands. A hat box.

Hannah wanted to die on the spot.

'Oh!' her mother said. 'I didn't know . . . oh my! It's Mr William. There's a surprise! I thought . . . '

Hannah wiped her hands down the sides of her skirt. She walked towards her mother, her heart in her mouth. Please, please, Ma, don't mention Ralph Lawlor — not with his brother, William, here with me, she thought.

Hannah was aware of William following her down the path.

They reached Hannah's mother and the hat box.

'It arrived an hour ago,' Hannah's ma said. 'From Perrett's. In Tavistock. Who could have sent it? But it *is* for you — the delivery man mentioned you by name. I've had a peek. Oh, it's beautiful. Don't you go touching it with those peaty hands, though.'

The words were tumbling out of her mother's mouth faster than the water tumbled over Becka Falls. And, before Hannah could stop her, she took off the lid. Inside — as Hannah had known it would be — nestled the hat she had so coveted when she'd been in Tavistock with Ralph.

'I'll be on my way,' William said.

He nodded to Hannah, and then her mother.

They both knew — she and William — who it was had sent her the hat.

5

There was a note in with the hat. *'Covet no more. A little token in thanks for your company.'*

'Company?' Edith said.

She made the word sound, Hannah thought, like something deeply disgusting and totally unpalatable.

'I was tricked, Ma,' Hannah said. 'Into going with him in the first place and into eating at The Bedford Hotel.'

'There? That place is for the nobs. But then, I suppose, Mr Ralph is a nob. And we all know how nobs get girls to . . . '

'Nothing happened, Ma,' Hannah interrupted. 'Honestly.'

Well, not then or afterwards she could have added, but didn't.

'Do I have your word on the Bible for that?'

'You do,' Hannah said. 'I'll fetch it, shall I?'

'No. If you're willing to promise on it, that'll do.'

'Didn't you wonder why I struggled to eat my supper that night?' Hannah asked. She wasn't at all sure her mother believed her, even though she'd said she'd swear on the Bible.

'Can't say as I did. But what's all this trickery of Mr Ralph's?'

So Hannah told her how Ralph had told Miss Pollyblank that his cousin, Daisy, would be acting as chaperone for the trip to Tavistock — except she hadn't.

'Daisy? Whenever have you heard me speak of a Miss Daisy? If there was any Daisy up at Huckstone House, then Annie Leigh would have mentioned it. And she hasn't. You never ought to have got in that carriage . . . '

'I know that now, Ma. But you seemed pleased enough when Mr Ralph called asking if I would dine with him.'

'Yes, and I didn't think you'd be

prancing about Tavistock with him like some trollop of a moll. I thought it was going to be in mixed company. Up at Huckstone House, perhaps. Something to do with Miss Pollyblank and the school. I know Mr Charles has always been generous, because . . . '

'Annie Leigh told you,' Hannah finished for her, wearily. She couldn't be bothered to refute that she was neither a trollop nor a moll. 'And it didn't escape my notice you were thrilled with the hat, in the garden just now. Couldn't sing its praises loudly enough.'

Hannah lifted the hat from the box, and placed it on her head. She went to the small mirror on the kitchen windowsill and peered at herself in the spotted glass. Even in bad light and with the glass making her look like she had a very bad case of the measles, it was still a wonderful hat.

'You're never going to wear it?' her mother said. 'Outside of here, I mean.'

'Well, I'm hardly likely to wear it indoors all day, am I?' Hannah spun round to face her mother. 'But the real answer is no — I'm not going to wear it. I shall return Mr Ralph's gift.'

'It's the right thing to do,' her mother said. 'Seeing as it seems Mr Ralph's calling on Miss Beth most days now, so I've 'eard. In the circumstances, you understand. But he's not going to be pleased.'

'No,' Hannah said, taking off the hat and replacing it carefully back in the box amongst the tissue. 'He's not.'

No more pleased than William had been seeing her receive it.

*　*　*

After lunch on Sunday, Hannah's mother had another of her funny turns. Hannah was all for going for Dr Tucker and be blowed with the expense. She had money saved and she was happy to dip into it to get her mother well.

But Edith wouldn't hear of it.

91

'Just you get yourself off to Dewer-bank and get that cream and butter made. I'll be all right. I'm sorry I won't be able to walk over to Huckstone House with you afterwards to return the hat. You'll have to go on your own.'

'I won't,' Hannah said. 'I'll think of something else.'

The thought of William being there, witness to her returning a gift from his brother, was more than she could bear. What might Ralph have told William that Hannah had done to warrant such a gift? She'd explained about the kiss and William had seemed happy to accept her explanation. Would he now think she'd lied about that?

'I just hope Beth Hannaford hasn't got to hear about it,' Edith said.

So do I, Hannah thought, as she made to leave for Dewerbank. So do I.

* * *

'Hannah French, I want a word with you.'

Hannah jumped as Beth Hannaford came into the dairy; she'd never been known to set foot in the place before. The butter Hannah had been patting up ready for the market slipped from between the paddles, and she grabbed for it, the greasy butter sliding against her bare hand. She only just managed to prevent it falling off the edge of the table.

'And don't waste that butter. You know my mother hates clumsy dairymaids.' Beth Hannaford glared at her, arms folded across her waist.

The other two dairymaids had stopped work and were staring open-mouthed.

'What do you want me for, Miss Beth?' Hannah said, although she had a sick feeling in the pit of her stomach it had something to do with Ralph Lawlor.

'Alone,' Beth Hannaford said. 'You two,' she pointed at the younger girls, 'can take a ten minute break. Over in the stables.'

'Yes, Miss,' they said in unison. And fled.

Hannah took a deep breath.

'Do you have issue with my dairying?' she asked.

'I think you know it's not that.'

'I know nothing until you tell me what it is you want to speak to me about,' Hannah said.

Hannah wasn't going to let Beth Hannaford see that she was quaking inside. She wasn't going to be intimidated by the acid-tongued miss if she could help it. If anything, Beth was even more spiteful than her mother, and that was saying something.

'Not what, but who.'

'*Whom*,' Hannah said, automatically correcting Beth's poor grammar. It was something she did every day at the school, but she'd give anything not to have said it now because Beth Hannaford looked as though she might explode with rage. She'd probably get the sack.

'Oh, yes,' Beth said, in a snide voice.

'I was quite forgetting you have to work at the school as well to make ends meet. Who? Whom? What does it matter?'

Quite a lot, Hannah thought, if you think you'll make the right wife for Ralph Lawlor.

'I apologise. I ought not to have said that.'

'The same as you ought not to have dined alone with Ralph Lawlor at The Bedford Hotel? I'd like to hear it from your own lips that it was you who was seen with Ralph.'

'If he said it was me, then it was,' Hannah said.

'Ah, but he didn't. Someone my informant thought was you was seen entering a private dining room. But since you now admit . . . '

'I can't deny it, Miss Beth,' Hannah said. 'But I was duped into going there.'

'A likely story.'

'It's the truth!'

'I simply don't believe you. You offered him the comforts of your body, no doubt, in exchange.'

'I most certainly did not!' Hannah was screaming now. She didn't care who heard her.

'The blame lies squarely with you. Men are weak where women throwing themselves at them are concerned. Ralph has been showering me with gifts — a precursor to a proposal if ever there was one,' Beth Hannaford said, a self-satisfied smile playing around her lips. 'I can forgive him one little weakness.'

And you'll be lucky if it is just the one when, and if, you become Mrs Lawlor, Hannah thought. Because I, too, was given a gift, she wanted to say, but didn't. What would Beth say about that if she knew? Although, unlike Beth, Hannah had been under no illusion that Ralph saw it as a precursor to a proposal in her case.

'So, you see, Miss French,' Beth said, 'why it simply isn't appropriate that you work here any more. Or your mother. This has been the second Sunday running your mother has been ill. We need healthy workers here, and reliable ones. I'll get . . . '

'You can't! You can't do that! My mother knew nothing of my journey to Tavistock with Mr Ralph. Or the dining. I only told her a short while ago. And as for being ill, well I'm sure it's just the change of season . . . '

'Enough. I neither want your ailing mother, nor sluts like you . . . '

'You'll take that back!' Hannah said. 'And what's more, I'll take my orders from your mother or your father, not you!'

Beth Hannaford clapped her hands together and laughed.

'Then you shall hear it.'

And with that, Mrs Hannaford came into the dairy. She had two cards in her hand. She gave them to Hannah.

'Go,' Mrs Hannaford said, putting an arm around Beth's shoulders. 'I heard everything, Hannah. But if you're wise, you will speak of none of this to anyone. Especially not to Ralph Lawlor.

Promise me that.'

'I'll go,' Hannah said. 'But I'll promise nothing.'

* * *

Sunday lunch, served by an even slower than usual Mrs Leigh, was an agonising wait until it was over for William.

On the journey to church in Tavistock in the carriage — Ralph holding the reins, while William sat in the back with their uncle — William had replayed the scene in his head when Hannah's mother had come out of the cottage with the hat box. Perrett's. Tavistock. Delivered for Hannah. Ralph had admitted to dining with someone in Tavistock. It had to be Hannah. So much for the kiss they'd shared being because Ralph had caught Hannah unawares. He wanted to believe her, but could he? His brother was capable of being extremely devious, though; he always had been even as a child.

What might Ralph have done to —

or with — Hannah in Tavistock? And what was a worse thought was what Hannah might have been so very keen to do with Ralph. Ralph would have no honourable intentions towards Hannah, that was for sure, because he'd been paying for gifts — silver-backed brushes, a diamanté brooch, gloves — to be delivered to Beth Hannaford, charging the accounts to his uncle.

'I'll retire, boys,' their uncle said at last, when the remains of lunch had been cleared away. 'If someone could help me to my room.'

'Your turn,' Ralph said to William. 'I'm going out.'

'Not just yet,' William said, barring his exit from the room. 'It's your turn. You were out all of yesterday. Back in the early hours . . . '

'You're not my keeper,' Ralph snapped.

'What? What's that, boys?' Charles Lawlor said. He was becoming increasingly deaf as well as blind.

'Ralph is just going to show you to your room, Uncle,' William said, speaking loudly and slowly.

And I am going to wait until his return and then I want some answers.

He didn't have long to wait. William resisted the urge to ask his brother if he'd thrown their uncle onto the bed and left him.

'Be quick about it, whatever it is you have to say,' Ralph said.

'Tavistock. Perrett's. A blue hat. Hannah French. Quick enough for you?'

'Ah, so you found out about that?' Ralph said, with a smirk. 'Perrett's is there for anyone with the means to buy hats.'

'But not if they pay for them — against his knowledge — from their uncle's account. Along with other things. Silver hair brushes . . . I won't go on.'

William waved a bundle of invoices at Ralph.

Ralph shrugged.

'He's hardly likely to know, is he?' Ralph jerked a thumb towards the upper floor.

'That's not the point, and you know it. I . . . '

'The point is,' Ralph said, striding across the room to stand nose-to-nose with William, 'that you are as jealous as hell that I've had the delightful company of the beautiful Miss French. And a kiss. One gem of a kiss . . . '

'Hannah explained that.'

'Did she say how weak at the knees it made her? Did she?' Ralph said. 'Not that one kiss means a marriage proposal is on the horizon. To which end, I do believe Miss Beth Hannaford is awaiting my attendance to take her for a drive — chaperoned, of course, which was something Hannah French was without.'

William ignored his brother's inference to Hannah's morals.

'Not before we've gone over these accounts,' William said. 'And not before everything purchased for your own ends is put on your account and not our uncle's. It might take some time.'

★   ★   ★

Hannah raced home for the hat. To cross the moor, as the crow flew, was quicker but she couldn't risk stumbling over tussocks of grass, or catching her foot in a rabbit hole. She went along the road.

'Ma!' she shouted, bursting in through the back door.

But no answering call came. Where was she? Her heart pounding now, Hannah took the small flight of stairs to the upper level two at a time. Her mother's bedroom door was open but she wasn't lying on her bed. Neither was she in Hannah's room, when she looked.

The privy then. Hannah made her way downstairs again, snatched the hat box from the table in the sitting-room and waited what she considered a suitable length of time for her mother to return from the privy. When she didn't put in an appearance after five minutes — five minutes when Hannah knew she was wasting time — she went outside and knocked tentatively on the privy door.

'Ma?'

No answer. Hannah lifted the latch. And it was with relief she saw the privy was empty. Resisting the urge to go off into flights of fancy about where her mother could be, Hannah decided she had merely gone for a short stroll somewhere for some fresh air.

So, the hat box held firmly in her hands, Hannah again raced along the road. This time, Huckstone House was her destination.

* * *

Ralph Lawlor came running down the front steps of Huckstone House as Hannah, very hot and breathless from running, arrived. He had a serious expression on his face, and he kept pushing a hand back through his hair as though concerned about something. But that serious look turned to one of pure displeasure when he saw Hannah.

'What the hell are *you* doing here?' he said, lips taught as wires.

'I've come to return this.'

Hannah walked forward and held the hat box out towards him.

'Stupid little fool,' Ralph said. 'There might have been more where that came from, if only you'd had the sense to use discretion.'

'I don't want more. I didn't see it, for one moment — the way Miss Beth sees the gifts you give her — as a precursor to a proposal.'

'Have you been talking to Miss Beth about this?' He banged the top of the box with a fist, before snatching it from her.

'No. But someone saw us, you and I, going into the dining room of The Bedford Hotel. And they've reported back.'

Ralph Lawlor spat out a word no gentleman would say, and certainly not in front of a lady. Hannah wondered if Beth Hannaford knew just what sort of man she was so very keen to marry. Yes, Ralph had good looks. And money. And for a moment she'd been stupid enough herself to be taken in by all of it. But not any more.

'Out of my way!'

Ralph Lawlor pushed Hannah roughly. Knocked off balance by the sudden action, Hannah knew she was going to fall. Anger and fright made her scream. Very loudly. Ralph kicked out at her and his boot caught her a stinging blow on her thigh.

'Shut up!'

Hannah screamed some more. Terrified now.

Then came the sound of a door being thrown back against a wall, and she heard William shout: 'Ralph! What the hell do you think you're doing?'

'This bitch you seem so keen on, is here making trouble.'

'I'm not a bitch, thank you!' Hannah said, getting to her feet. She clutched at her thigh, which was beginning to throb where Ralph had kicked it. 'Miss Beth has given me and my ma our cards because you tricked me into going to Tavistock with you and someone saw. I don't want to work at Dewerbank ever again, but Ma has to. We can't afford the rent without those wages. At her age, Ma's not likely to get another position. This is all your fault. You *have* to ask Mrs Hannaford to take my mother back.'

'A very pretty speech,' Ralph said. 'But I do no-one's bidding, least of all yours.'

'Back in the house!' William said. He grabbed Ralph roughly by the elbow with one hand. 'Are you all right to follow, Hannah?'

'I am. But I don't want to.'

'And neither do I!' Ralph yelled. He struggled to free himself from William, but the hat box was an encumbrance.

He threw it on the ground, kicking it away from him. 'You're welcome to the bitch!'

'You'll take that slur back,' William said, his voice cool and cold and — Hannah thought — determined.

'Make me,' Ralph said.

And then to Hannah's utter amazement, they began to fight. Although Ralph was the more wiry of the brothers, he was no match for William. Within seconds, William had his brother pinned to the ground by his shoulders, unable to move.

'Enough?' William asked.

He stepped away from Ralph, who scrambled to his feet, retrieved the hat box and ran for the stables.

Hannah didn't know what to say. She stood looking at William, wondering why she had ever considered she might prefer Ralph over him. But would he want her now?

'You look shocked, Hannah,' William said. 'Will you come into the house? Some brandy for your shock perhaps?

Or a cup of tea? And then I'll see you safely home.'

'Just a cup of tea,' Hannah said. 'Thank you. That will be lovely.'

★   ★   ★

Hannah was glad of William's help going home. Her thigh was stiff now from Ralph's kick and she knew that when she looked, there would be a bruise. As Ralph had taken the carriage, William had had no option but to take the pony and trap.

In fact, Hannah preferred it to the carriage. She could see more for a start than through the small — and rather dirty — carriage window. And she was beyond caring now who saw her riding on a Sunday beside William. No doubt, Ralph would spread all sorts of tales about her — or Beth Hannaford would.

'I'll see you safely inside,' William said.

He jumped down from the trap and secured a tether to the hook beside the front door of Hannah's cottage. Then he helped Hannah to the ground.

'Ow,' she said. 'I hurt it when I fell . . . '

'And not only that. Ralph kicked you — I saw him. Hannah, I'm sorry . . . '

'Don't,' Hannah said. 'Please don't apologise for your brother. That has to come from him. Thank you for bringing me home. I won't keep you any longer.'

William nodded.

'My brother will be taken to account for his actions,' he said.

'But my ma's position at Dewerbank?' Hannah said. 'The Hannafords *must* take her back. They must. We can't manage . . . '

'I'll see what I can do,' William said. 'One way or another.'

And then, to Hannah's surprise, he reached for her hand and raised it to his lips; kissed it — his lips warm and dry on the back of her hand.

'I'll be in touch,' he said.

He unhooked the rein and jumped back into the trap. One flick of the rein on the pony's flank and they were off. Hannah watched until they were out of sight.

Hannah pushed open the front door of Hillside Cottage.

'Ma, I'm back and . . . '

And then she stopped. A pair of men's boots was placed neatly just inside the door and the owner of them was sitting on the settle beside her mother, who looked far from ill now.

Just what was going on?

6

'You lied to me, Ma!' Hannah raged at her mother after the owner of the boots — Edward Dyer — had left. 'You made an almighty fuss about me going unchaperoned to Tavistock with Ralph Lawlor and being given gifts, and there you were, as cosy as you like, with Mr Dyer!'

'You don't understand. You see . . . '

'I understand well enough, Ma. There's one rule for you and another for me, so it seems.'

'I'm a widow. And I don't need a chaperone at my age either,' Edith French said.

'And you don't have to be so underhand about it all. I suppose he was here last Sunday afternoon when you had a *funny turn*, was he?'

Edith nodded.

'I didn't know how else I was going

to see him. He works in the day all week, same as I do. Saturdays he takes flowers to his wife's grave and he has to walk all the way to Yelverton to do it. But you must have noticed how he sits close by in the church during the service.'

'I can't say I have,' Hannah said. 'I was concentrating more on the prayers and the sermons than seeing who was sitting where. Seems you weren't though, doesn't it?'

Now she thought about it, she could remember her ma talking to Edward Dyer after the service more than a few times. She hadn't taken much notice then, because usually Miss Pollyblank was intent on pinning Hannah down to some lengthy discussion about what art project Hannah could get the children interested in.

'He's been a widower a long time, Hannah. Longer 'n I've been a widow and that's been long enough.'

Hannah saw the glisten of unshed tears in her mother's eyes.

'Oh, Ma,' Hannah said, all her anger seeping out of her now. 'I don't begrudge you the friendship, honestly I don't. I just wish you hadn't been so secretive about it, that's all.'

She went to kiss her mother's cheek but Edith flapped a hand at her.

'No need to get soppy on me. You and me've never gone in for hugs nor kisses, no reason to start now. What brings you home so early anyway?'

You've never wanted to hug or kiss *me*, Hannah wanted to say. And she'd bet her last sixpence that her ma and Edward had kissed and hugged plenty, if their guilty faces had been anything to go by when Hannah had come home unexpectedly.

Hannah took a deep breath.

'You gave me a huge shock just now sitting there with Edward Dyer, and now I'm afraid *I've* got a shock for *you* — Miss Beth found out that I'd been to Tavistock with Ralph Lawlor. Seems he *is* courting her, and she thinks a proposal is imminent. She gave me my cards. Or rather, her mother did. Yours, too.'

'The sack?' Edith said, hands flying to her face. 'You mean we've got the sack, the both of us?'

'Yes. But I've been to see Mr Ralph and demanded he do something about it — that the Hannafords take *you* back at least, seeing as he tricked me into going to Tavistock. William brought me back in the pony and trap just now. He says he's going to see what he can do about it.'

'But if he don't, then what'll us do? We can barely afford the rent between us — you doing two jobs and all. And there's no good me asking Edward for help, 'cos he's no better off than we are; there's not a spare halfpenny between the lot of us.'

Edith began to cry.

'I'll put the kettle on, Ma,' Hannah said. She limped to the draining board where a jug of water always stood, full and ready for just such a purpose. 'A cup of tea is what we both need.'

'What's wrong with your leg?'

'Ralph Lawlor kicked me. But don't you dare breathe a word of it to anyone. Especially not to Annie Leigh.'

'He what?'

'You heard.'

'Well, best make that the last time you are ever alone with a Lawlor, then. His brother'll be just like him, you see if he isn't!'

Hannah banged the full kettle down on the range, and said nothing. William was nothing like his brother. She put the back of her hand where William had kissed her to her cheek. If she never got another kiss from William, then she would always cherish the memory.

* * *

On May Day the children, dressed in their Sunday best, danced around a maypole set up on the village green. Mary Narracott was crowned May Queen and there was a parade through the town. Hannah had had the devil's own job to keep the children from dirtying their Sunday best by playing too roughly on the grass or smearing it with the jelly and cake tea the vicar had provided. A shower of rain had sent them all scuttling back to the school.

'I'll be off, Miss Pollyblank,' Hannah said, 'if there's nothing else you want me for.'

'Well, there is something,' Miss Pollyblank said, twisting her hands over and over.

Hannah made to take off her coat. But Miss Pollyblank stopped her.

'No, no. You can go in a moment. It's nothing I need you to stay here for.'

'Then what is it?' Hannah asked. She could see Miss Pollyblank was uncomfortable.

'I've had a letter. I won't say from whom, but the contents have alarmed me. It's come to my notice you were seen dining in Tavistock with a man. Alone. If that is true, then I'm not at all sure you are the right person to be in charge of children.'

Hannah sighed. She had a good idea who had written the letter; Mrs Hannaford, or possibly Miss Beth.

'I dined at The Bedford Hotel with Mr Lawlor. Mr Ralph. You instructed me to go to Tavistock with him to buy stationery and books for the children. He tricked both you and me when he said his cousin, Daisy, would be acting as chaperone. He has no cousin, Daisy, and there was no chaperone either. I could hardly have run away from him in Tavistock and walked home in the dark.'

'You were with him after dark?'

The same things can happen in daylight as they can in the dark, Hannah wanted to say. Her mother had said that to her many times when she'd warned her about the devious ways of men.

'It *would* have been pitch black if I'd walked the nine miles home, if I hadn't acquiesced and dined with him. As it happened, the light was fading fast when he stopped his carriage at The

Saracen's Head for me to get out.'

'Yes, yes,' Miss Pollyblank said. 'But I'm in a quandary now. The writer of the letter says they will withdraw their very generous donations to my school if you are not given your orders to leave. I . . .'

'But that's preposterous! So unfair!'

Hannah waited for Miss Pollyblank to chide her for interrupting. Or to say that life isn't fair, which is what she always said to the children if they complained of some unfairness — real or imagined.

But she didn't. She smiled at Hannah instead.

'A woman scorned, I would say, Hannah.' She picked up the letter from her desk and waved it at Hannah, then put it firmly in the pocket of her skirt. 'In the circumstances, I will do no such thing. I am sure there must be other benefactors in the area. You may go.'

Hannah dropped a small curtsey.

'Thank you. Good day, Miss Pollyblank.'

Oh yes, Hannah thought, as she made her way home. Beth Hannaford was a woman scorned indeed. And she had a feeling she hadn't heard the last of her.

★ ★ ★

'I've had a word with Uncle,' Ralph said. 'I've explained how, now that we've had to close the copper mine through loss of demand and it's only the quarry making money, we must stop our donations to the village school.'

'We?' William said. 'I didn't know that you'd paid out a penny of your own. And as for making money . . .'

'That little refrain?' Ralph interrupted. 'I suppose you've been poring over the quarry's accounts. Better you let your eyes roam over some pretty miss than pages of figures, I say.'

'My eyes, maybe,' William said. 'But not my feet.'

'Ah, Miss French, I presume. It was a reflex action. She was screaming and I wanted her to stop so as not to alert the servants.'

'Is that how you justify your animal actions?'

Ralph didn't respond instantly. He bit his bottom lip, staring into the distance as though deep in thought.

'I'll ask you a question now,' Ralph said at last. 'Miss French. Is she ever far from your thoughts?'

'No,' William said, in all honesty.

He'd started carving a head and shoulders of her out of granite, even if it was the hardest of stones to sculpt. He had it hidden down at the quarry, working on it after all the men had gone home.

'I'm beginning to regret the day I met Miss Hannah French. And so, dear brother, might you one day.'

'And *you*,' William said, pointing a finger at Ralph, 'lay one finger on her — never mind your boots — and you'll have me to answer to. And it won't be just a restraining hold on your shoulders next time. Understand?'

'Perfectly. But it doesn't alter the fact we can't afford to make donations to the school, where . . . '

' . . . where Hannah works. Is that what you were going to say?'

'I had an adjective or two to put in front of her name, but yes, that's the gist of it.'

Ralph walked to the back door, lifting his riding crop from the hook on the wall.

'Withdraw what you will with your petty actions,' William said to his retreating figure. 'I won't hesitate to reinstate it.'

'Then you're a fool. A lovesick fool. She's more trouble than she's worth, is Hannah French. Needs teaching a lesson or two.'

And, without giving William a chance to respond, he was gone.

★ ★ ★

The following Sunday, Ralph Lawlor came to St Michael's. He walked, arm-in-arm with Beth Hannaford, behind her parents, to the Hannaford pew.

Sitting at the back of the church, Hannah's mother nudged her.

'I saw,' Hannah whispered.

Edith looked around — searching out Edward Dyer, Hannah guessed. He hadn't arrived yet, although her mother had said that he had sent a note to say he would call on her at two o'clock.

All through the service, Hannah was unable to take her eyes off Beth Hannaford's hat — the very same hat Ralph had given Hannah. Hannah wanted to giggle, wondering what excuse Ralph might have given Beth about the battered state of the box. But he would have come up with some lie, she knew that. And what would Beth think if she knew she'd been given a hat that Hannah had returned unwanted?

Hannah sat, hands folded neatly in her lap, waiting for the Reverend Toop to announce the banns that Beth Hannaford and Ralph Lawlor were to wed, but no reading of banns came.

'Looks like he's got his feet firmly under the table,' Hannah's mother said afterwards, as they walked home in the sunshine.

The Hannaford party drove by in a carriage at that moment. Not the one Ralph had driven her to Tavistock in. A much smarter carriage, Hannah couldn't help noticing. And the horses were better groomed, too.

'Doesn't it,' Hannah said.

'And I ain't got my job back, neither,' Edith said. 'Usually her ladyship looks over as she passes by and nods at me, but 'er didn't today.'

'I noticed,' Hannah said. 'No great loss.'

''Tis to me with no job. I've had no luck finding another, neither. Don't look like Mr William's kept his promise about doing something about it with the Hannafords, do it?'

'No,' Hannah said. 'But maybe it's taking time.'

'Mebbe,' her mother said. 'But I ain't

'olding me breath that he'll win one over on the Hannafords.'

'What's for lunch?' Hannah said as she pushed open the front door.

'Bread and scrape,' Edith said, a grin on her face. 'And a lot more of it if things don't improve around 'ere. Now get it down yer and off out somewhere, 'cos I'm having company.'

* * *

Hannah looked up from her reading, alerted by the sound of a skylark flying high in alarm at something, or someone, coming too close to its nest.

William. He was walking towards her, a bag slung over one shoulder and a small easel clutched firmly with both hands in front of him. And he was smiling at her.

'Your mother told me you'd probably be here.'

'You called at the house?'

'I did. I had news to impart.'

'Good or bad?' Hannah asked, as

William placed his easel and bag on the ground then sat down beside her.

'Good, I hope. I haven't been able to get your mother's job back for her with the Hannafords but I have been able to find her work. With Dr Tucker. I was at university with his brother, Simon, and Dr Tucker came up to take us out to dinner a time or two. Not that I've seen anything of Simon since I've been back, I've been too busy at the quarry. Anyway, that's all by the by. Dr Tucker needs help. Just three days a week. He needs someone to clean after the day's surgery. Your mother seemed delighted when I told her.'

'I expect she was,' Hannah said. 'Oh, thank you so very much for doing that for her.'

Hannah had to wrap her arms across her waist to stop herself from flinging them around William to give him a kiss on the cheek for his kindness.

'I'm pleased to have been able to help. But I have to tell you she was even more delighted when I told her I couldn't stop more than a few minutes.'

William grinned broadly at her.

'Edward Dyer's arrived then?' she said.

'He has indeed. So I thought you might be in need of some company.'

'And glad of it,' Hannah said. 'I'm sorry, you know, about the hat and that I was foolish enough to get in a carriage alone with your brother, although nothing happened that . . . '

'You don't have to explain. There's no need. I'm the one who's sorry. I ought to have warned you about him and his underhand ways sooner. Obviously, talk of his reputation hadn't reached you.'

'No,' Hannah said.

She wondered if William could tell that she'd been attracted to Ralph initially. Certainly when Ralph had kissed her, she had kissed him back very enthusiastically. Now, though, Hannah realised that with lots of experience at kissing, Ralph probably knew what techniques — if kissing was a technique and not just a feeling; she wouldn't know, she had so little experience — to apply to stir a woman's feelings so that it felt as though her bones were melting.

'It's I who should apologise. I'm ashamed that a brother of mine could kick a lady.'

'Shall we stop apologising to one another?' Hannah laughed.

'What do you suggest we do instead?' William asked.

'You could paint, or draw, or whatever it is you have come to do,' Hannah said quickly.

'I came to see you. I only brought all this in case I didn't find you.'

'Oh,' Hannah said, startled. 'That's a lovely thing to say. I'm flattered.'

She felt herself flush. But William affected not to notice. He took a sketchpad from his bag and opened it, giving Hannah time for the flush to fade perhaps?

Hannah watched, in silence, as he began to sketch a sprig of gorse. The early sun had caused all the gorse buds to burst open and the air was full of its honey scent. William took a tin of watercolour paint and began to colour the sketch. He worked in silence, although it was a comfortable silence between them. Hannah read a few pages of her book.

'I can't believe sometimes,' she said, as she finished the chapter, 'that we've not encountered one another more, seeing as you have lived with your uncle since . . . '

Oh dear. What to say now? William and Ralph's parents had died within weeks of one another with typhus, caught on a holiday to Rome, so local gossip had it.

'Since our parents died is what you were going to say, isn't it?'

'Yes.'

'It was so long ago now, and it grieves me to say I hardly remember them. Our uncle, childless as he and his late wife were, put us both in boarding school just as soon as he could. And then he put us both through university. So it's not surprising you've not seen much of either of us until now.'

'Did you like boarding school and university?' Hannah asked. 'Do women go?'

'Yes to both questions. Although neither the school nor the university were mixed, as village schools are.'

'No forced country dancing, whether you wanted to or not?' Hannah laughed. 'The girls like it well enough, but not the boys.'

'No country dancing,' William said. 'But at university I did learn to dance. I can affect a fairly passable waltz when the occasion demands. Although there's not a lot of demand on the moor.'

'The waltz,' Hannah said dreamily.

'I could show you,' William said. He stood up and turned a complete circle. 'No-one to see us. This piece of flat grass should be perfect.'

He reached out a hand for Hannah to pull her to her feet.

She took the hand, and William

clasped her firmly but gently.

'I'll have to hold you quite closely,' he said.

With that, he took Hannah's left hand and placed it on his right upper arm. Then he clasped Hannah's right hand in his left. Putting his own right hand in the small of her back, he pulled her gently towards him, as close as he could, but their bodies not touching.

'I'll guide you with the movement of my body,' he said.

How good it felt to Hannah to be held so gently, so firmly. To have William smiling down at her. He gave brief, but precise, instructions about where she should place her feet. It seemed confusing at first, but she soon mastered it. The area of grass wasn't large, so William had to whirl her round so they could dance back the other way. As they danced, their feet crushed emerging buds of chamomile which scented the air with their sweet, herbal aroma. How wonderful it all felt.

William began to sing — something

about light and eyes and crystals and midnight; a song Hannah hadn't heard before. William had a wonderful singing voice, better than any of the men in the choir at St. Michael's.

Their dance became slower and slower. They came to a standstill and Hannah felt the pressure of William's lips on the top of her head.

'I'm going to have to go now, Hannah,' William said, his voice husky.

'Me, too,' Hannah said, although she thought her heart might burst with the happiness of the moment.

'But in opposite directions.' William's face became serious. 'You're not afraid out here on the moor alone? With the prison being just over there, I mean.'

'The prison?' Hannah said. 'Why, it's never bothered me, no. I've grown up with it. I see the prisoners being escorted to work at the prison quarry or on the prison farm most days, but always they look away from me. And if they don't, then a warder is quick to remind them of their manners.'

'Good,' William said. 'Will you be here again soon, Hannah?'

'I try to be. With the evenings so light now, it seems a crime not to after being cooped up in school all day.'

'Then I hope to see you here. Perhaps I could draw you?'

'I'd like that,' Hannah said. 'Thank you for the dance.'

'The pleasure was all mine,' William said. He reached for her hand and raised it to his lips. He kissed the palm this time, not the back of it. Hannah thought she might melt with the delight of the feelings the gesture created in her.

After William had disappeared into the distance, she pressed her palm — where he had kissed it — against her lips.

* * *

Hannah was halfway home and had just entered a gulley between two rocky outcrops when she saw him. Ralph

Lawlor. His horse was nibbling grass and Ralph stood, leaning against a rock, arms folded and grim-faced.

'Everything comes to he who waits,' he said.

Hannah froze. She'd walked this way a thousand times and never seen a living soul in this particular spot before. Her mouth went dry and when she went to speak, she found she couldn't. Her heart rate increased alarmingly and she could feel her pulse at the side of her neck.

'What do you want of me?' Hannah managed to croak out at last.

'Another kiss,' Ralph said. 'Willingly given, or . . .'

'No!' Hannah's hands flew to her face to cover her mouth.

Ralph laughed. He pushed himself away from the rock on which he was leaning and took a step towards her.

' . . . or otherwise.'

'How can you even think of such a thing?' Hannah asked. Her hands down by her sides now, she made balls of her fists, ready to punch Ralph Lawlor if she had to. 'You were in church this morning with the Hannafords. Sitting next to Miss Beth . . . '

'Stop!' Ralph said. 'I want to ask you a question.'

'I don't promise to answer it,' Hannah said.

'You're spirited, I'll say that,' Ralph laughed. 'I'll ask anyway. Did you enjoy the fine food and the wine, and all the things you could buy in the shops of Tavistock if only you had the money?'

Hannah pressed her lips together, refusing to answer.

'Oh, I think you did. And had you played your cards right, I could have given you those things — discreetly, of course. But not now. What I like even less in a woman than not knowing her place, is a woman who makes me look a fool in front of my brother. You need teaching a lesson, you do.'

And then it was as though everything happened in slow motion. Ralph leapt forward towards her, grabbed her roughly by the shoulder and pushed her towards the rocks. He was grabbing at her skirt with his free hand.

'Please . . . don't hurt . . . ' Hannah said, before her head hit granite and everything went black.

* * *

William reached the quarry, empty of workers now that he'd caught up with orders. Leaving Hannah had been hard. He'd known women at university — women from the ladies' colleges, with whom he and fellow students had fraternised — and he'd liked them well enough. Had known the bodies of one or two well enough, too. But none of them had filled his head and his heart the way Hannah French was filling it now. When she'd been in his arms, it had been the devil's own job not to kiss her the way he wanted to. A chaste kiss on the head had been nowhere near enough what his body was urging him to do.

Slowly, William made his way to where he'd hidden the carving he was making of Hannah's likeness. It was almost finished. He put his painting things down on the ground and pulled the stones away from the niche where he'd hidden his carving.

And then his heart gave a lurch. His carving was there all right, but in a hundred pieces.

Ralph. It had to be Ralph who had found it and ruined it.

And then William began to laugh. The sound echoed back at him from the cliff faces — 100 foot in some places — of the quarry. He laughed until the tears ran down his cheeks.

If Ralph thought that wrecking one sculpture was going to stop William making another, with all the granite there was on Dartmoor to work with, then he was the world's biggest fool.

7

Early Summer 1903

'Another jug of water, Hannah?' her mother said. 'You'll wash yourself away.'

I could never have enough water to wash Ralph Lawlor away, Hannah thought. She'd regained consciousness to find Ralph gone, and an ache in her lower body she thought she might die from. Thank God her head hadn't been cut, or her Ma would have had lots of questions; questions Hannah would never have been able to find the words to answer.

'It's the swaling, Ma,' Hannah lied. 'All that smoke coming off the dead bracken. The smitchey bits make my flesh creep.'

'Well, we can only pray Farmer Caunter puts an end to it soon. That's the third time you've been in the tub this week. The well'll run dry soon, to say nothing of the peat you'm burning to heat the water.'

'I'll cut more peat, Ma,' Hannah said. 'Before the winter.'

'Oh, that reminds me,' Edith said. 'The fairies must have come in the night. There's more peat piled up than ever you put there last week and the turf-iron was cleaned off and left by the back door.'

'Was it?' Hannah said.

'I just said, Hannah French,' Edith laughed. 'And I'd lay my last halfpenny down that it was Mr William what did it. He didn't much like it when he saw the 'at what his brother gave you, but he was keener 'n mustard to come and find you last Sunday when he called about the position he got me with Dr Tucker. I take back everything I said about 'n. He's as different from 'is brother as chalk is from cheese.'

Yes, Hannah thought, he is. But what if Ralph reported back what he had done to her? William wouldn't want her then, would he?

* * *

'Is something wrong, Miss French?' Miss Pollyblank asked.

'Wrong?' Hannah repeated. 'With what?'

'With you. Only I can't help noticing you've snapped at the children rather a lot this week. It's not like you to snap. You had little Robbie Stratton in tears on Wednesday. I know he can be a sensitive soul, but all the same . . . '

'Did I?' Hannah said.

She thought back to Wednesday. The weather had remained fine and she'd organised a game of tag for the children in the playground. She'd been glad to be out in the fresh air, if truth be told, instead of stuck indoors with images of Ralph Lawlor floating in and out of her mind.

'You did. And I can't help noticing your mind doesn't seem to be quite with us this week. I've had to repeat myself more than a few times when you've looked blankly at me.'

Miss Pollyblank sounded concerned rather than cross with her, and the woman's unexpected kindness made tears well behind Hannah's eyes.

'I'm sorry,' Hannah said. 'I'm a little tired, that's all. The change of season. And it's been so unseasonably warm.'

'And don't we all know it!' Miss Pollyblank said. 'The Carter children's clothes — always so damp on account of the hovel the poor mites live in — fair steamed in the heat coming in the classroom window.'

'Did they?' Hannah said.

'There you go again, Miss French, dear — questioning things as though you haven't fully understood. It's obvious something is ailing you and I'd like to be able to say you can take a day or two off to recover, but I'm afraid I can't.'

'No, of course not,' Hannah said. 'I'll try and get an early night tonight.'

Now William had so kindly cut peat without being asked, there'd be no need for her to go out and do it again just yet. She ought to thank him. She'd seen him on his horse riding towards the spot where they'd danced so happily together just a few short days ago, and she'd known he was going there in the hope of seeing her. But she hadn't been able to face him — not yet. If ever, now.

Hannah tried to stop a yawn from coming, but failed miserably.

'Going to bed the second you've had supper tonight wouldn't be too early,' Miss Pollyblank said.

Oh yes it would, Hannah wanted to say. The second she got into bed and lay her head on the pillow, Ralph Lawlor's angry, determined face would swim in front of her.

'Mr Ralph has withdrawn his uncle's patronage of our school,' Miss Pollyblank said suddenly. The sound of his name took Hannah's breath away and she coughed before taking in air again. 'As have Mr and Mrs Hannaford.' In a gesture that surprised Hannah, because Miss Pollyblank had never done it before, she laid a hand on her shoulder and patted it. 'I have a feeling that their actions are connected to you in some way, but I'm not going to ask what.' She smiled warmly at Hannah. 'But never fear, all is not lost. Mr William has promised me twice what the other two were giving put together.'

'He has?'

'Miss French,' Miss Pollyblank said, wagging a finger playfully at Hannah, 'I've a good mind to have Dr Tucker come and test your hearing!'

'No,' Hannah said quickly. 'There's no need. My hearing is perfectly fine.'

Even if the rest of me isn't, Hannah thought. And with her mother working for the doctor now, she probably wouldn't be able to consult him without Edith having the opportunity to look at her notes. She knew she ought to go and see the doctor to see if Ralph, in his roughness, had damaged her in any way. But perhaps, the fewer people who knew what had happened to her, the better it would be.

Hannah stifled another yawn.

'Off you go,' Miss Pollyblank said. 'I won't keep you a second longer.'

She began tidying papers and books on her desk, returning stray pencils to the pot.

Hannah had been dismissed.

* * *

On the 26th June, William went to London, although he was reluctant to do so. The company he worked for — Messrs. Arbuthnott and Struthers — had written requesting his presence at a board meeting. He'd taken three months' leave of absence to return to Huckstone House to sort out his uncle's affairs and he'd written to them to say he now wished to be released from his post, citing his uncle's failing sight and general degeneration with age, as reason. But they had been unwilling to accept his resignation.

He took one of the new electric trams to their plush offices. How far away Dartmoor seemed, with its horses and carts and traction engines.

'Could you not get a manager in?' Charles Arbuthnott asked.

William sat up straighter in his chair.

'No, Sir, I couldn't. The quarry's finances won't run to that at present. My uncle had to close the copper mine a year ago now, since copper is being mined more cheaply abroad.'

'Yes, yes. Hard times. But you have a brother, do you not?' Andrew Struthers joined the debate.

'I do. But I'm afraid he's far from reliable.'

There was more William could have said to further his case. The fact that Ralph had claimed for hundreds of pounds worth of powder for blasting at the quarry, yet William had been able to find invoices for only £60 worth, for a start. Just one of a number of discrepancies in the account-keeping he'd asked Ralph about and to which he'd been given evasive answers, if not downright lies.

'Would another £100 per annum on your salary encourage you to stay?' Andrew Struthers asked. He was reaching for his cheque book on the desk as he spoke. 'In advance . . . '

'It's kind of you, Sir,' William said. 'But no. I really am going to have to make my life back in Devon for the foreseeable future.'

With a foray into foreign parts — Italy and France had always held appeal for William — once he'd got to the bottom of what Ralph had been up to. Then he might be able to consider putting a manager in, over Ralph's head if needs be, and go. And how he'd love to take Hannah with him. But she seemed to be avoiding him lately. He'd lost count of the times he'd been to what she'd said was her favourite spot, and where he'd held her so closely in his arms and they'd danced together, but he hadn't even caught a glimpse of her.

She was still working at the school, because Miss Pollyblank had written to thank him for his donation for art supplies. '*Miss French will, I'm sure, be thrilled to know of this and will put the money to good use on the children's behalf*,' was what she'd said in her letter.

Just thinking of Hannah now, and how she'd looked — felt — in his arms, made him smile.

'Ah,' Charles Arbuthnott said, smiling. 'I think I'm reading between the lines now, Mr Lawlor. Correct me if I'm wrong, but I do believe there's a woman claiming your heart, is there not?'

Was he as transparent as that? Obviously so.

'Yes, Mr Arbuthnott,' William said. 'I do believe there is.'

★ ★ ★

Busy scraping some new potatoes Miss Pollyblank had given her from the little patch of garden she managed to cultivate behind high stone walls, sheltered from the winds that whipped across the moor, Hannah jumped as someone rapped on the door.

Her mother had gone to Plymouth on the train from Princetown with Edward Dyer. They'd asked her to go with them, but Hannah had declined. Who wanted to be a wallflower?

She wished she *had* gone now. She sent up a silent prayer that the caller wasn't Ralph Lawlor. Reluctantly, she walked towards the door and pulled back the bolt.

'Letter for you, Miss French,' Fred Adams, the local postman, said.

Hannah took the proffered letter.

'Not your birthday, Miss Hannah, is it?'

'No,' Hannah said. She turned the envelope over and over in her hand. Who was it from? William? She'd never seen his handwriting; only his drawing and his painting.

'Shame,' Fred said, winking at her.

'Only I might have given you a birthday kiss if it were!'

'Cheek,' Hannah said, rustling up a smile for the kindly man. She knew he wouldn't dare do any such thing.

' 'Tis a card, though,' Fred said.

'How can you tell?'

'Stiffer 'n paper, see. Heavier and all. More postage.' Fred Adams tapped the stamp on Hannah's envelope with an index finger. 'From a beau, is it?'

'Don't you have other letters to deliver?' Hannah admonished him.

'That means it is!' Fred said, and scuttled off, pulling his pushbike from the front hedge of Hillside Cottage.

Hannah shut the door. Put the bolt across. The back door was bolted, too, whenever she was alone in the house. Just in case . . . Hannah didn't allow herself to think beyond those three words.

Carefully, she opened the flap of the envelope, fingered out a sheet of stiff card. Stiff card with a painting stuck on it. William had painted a scene of her favourite spot. A scene of a couple, arms around one another, dancing in the setting sun.

Hannah gulped back tears, as she turned the painting over.

'It could be my imagination, but it seems to me you are avoiding me. I thought we were growing closer but perhaps I imagined that, too? If you want no more of me, then I hope you will, accept this painting as a memory of what was, for me, a magical moment. I need no painting — that sweet memory will be with me forever.'

Hannah kissed the words William had written.

'Oh, William,' she said, her voice aching with sorrow. 'I want more of you, I really do. But for your brother . . . '

Hannah let the tears flow then. Ralph Lawlor had done more than violate her body; he had left her with child.

How long would she be able to hide the evidence?

* * *

'So,' Ralph said, as he and William were waiting to be called into dinner, 'the wanderer returns. For the time being . . . '

'I've been back a week, as well you know. And I might as well tell you now,' William said, 'I've resigned my position.'

'Idiot!' Ralph said. 'There's barely enough profit from the quarry to fund the two of us.'

'There might be,' William said, 'if you were less dishonest in your dealings. I've explained the position to Uncle Charles . . . '

'That deaf old . . . '

'Don't be disrespectful! Let me finish. We are both to sign cheques now — you and me. And every shipment of stone out will be countersigned by the other, too.'

'You've done this behind my back,' Ralph said.

'I might have consulted you, had you been at home. But you almost never are these days. Dewerbank seems to be your second home.'

'God, Will, but it's not only our uncle who's blind. You are, too. I'm going to have to spell it out for you, aren't I?' Ralph went to the dresser and poured a very generous slug of whisky into a tumbler. He wheeled round to face William, the whisky slopping dangerously near the edge of the glass as he did so. 'Miss Beth's an only child. The Hannafords are wealthy. And — so I've heard — her father is far from well. Losing weight. Dr Tucker's arranged for him to see some consultant up in Exeter. Are you following this, Will?'

'Get on with it,' William said.

Although he knew what Ralph was going to say.

'So, the Hannaford fortune added to ours — once uncle goes to meet his maker — and we'd be . . . '

'You scheming bastard! Are you saying you'd marry Miss Beth for her fortune?'

'It's been known,' Ralph laughed. 'And besides, she's very accommodating is Beth, the way she opens the sash window and lets me in her bedroom of a night.'

The maid knocked at the door then and told William and Ralph that dinner was ready.

'Five minutes,' William told her.

'Very well, Mr William,' the maid said and scurried off.

'And when we've eaten,' William said, 'we're both going to the quarry to see the shipment of carved bridge corbels loaded onto the wagon for the traction engine to haul down to Plymouth.'

'Are they finished already?'

'If you'd been around, you'd know they are. I've done most of them.'

And it had meant he'd had no time before the light went to search out Hannah reading somewhere on the moor.

'Can't that wait until morning?'

'No. The evenings are still light. It made sense to make use of the traction engine in conjunction with some stonework which Merrivale Quarry are shipping out.'

And with that William marched off to the dining-room.

* * *

The last week of the school term was rushing by faster than all the others, Hannah thought. Most of the children — the sons and daughters of prison warders mostly — were excited at the thought of being free from the constraints of high collars for the boys, and starched aprons for the girls.

'Oi 'ates whortleberry picking, Miss,' Jane Stokes said, smiling up at Hannah.

'Why's that, Jane?' Hannah asked.

She carried on rinsing out paintbrushes, an action now that always brought William to mind. How she missed him. Annie Leigh had passed on the news that William was down at the quarry every day, stopping until the light was gone, loading stone. Or carving. And Mrs Leigh had also passed on the news that Ralph escaped to Dewerbank and Beth Hannaford as often as he could, leaving William to do the bulk of the work.

''Cos it stains your fingers worse 'an anything, Miss. And my ma scrubs at 'em with carbolic soap and it stings like buggery.'

'Jane!' Hannah said, stifling a laugh because the word sounded so funny coming from such young lips. And the child was right. Whortleberries did stain the skin more than any other fruit Hannah knew of. 'Such language.'

'Sorry, Miss, but it do. Will you be out whortling, Miss?' Jane asked. 'I saw 'ee there last summer holidays.'

Will I? Hannah thought. So far her ma hadn't suspected that all was not well with Hannah. Thank goodness she hadn't been afflicted with the morning sickness as some were, because surely her ma would have noticed then. But her waist was thickening slightly. She'd have to move the button on her skirt soon.

'You haven't answered, Miss,' Jane prompted. She tipped her head to one side, studying Hannah with her sloe black eyes.

Hannah tucked a strand of curly hair back behind the child's ear.

'And you, little miss, haven't washed those jam jars out nearly well enough.'

A lump rose in Hannah's throat and she thought it might choke her. Jane Stokes was a beautiful child, and always so sunny-natured, despite the fact she had to walk three miles each way to school and back every day in all weathers.

Am I carrying a girl? Hannah wondered. And if she was, was she going to be able to keep her to see her grow into someone as delightful as little Jane?

* * *

Hannah was always paid a retainer in the school holidays. Just a third of her normal wage, but enough so she and her mother didn't starve. At least Edith hadn't been complaining so much of late now that she only had three days a week at Dr Tucker's surgery instead of the five full, and two half, days she'd had at Dewerbank, because Dr Tucker was paying her handsomely.

Rather too handsomely, Hannah thought. Did William have a hand in that?

She'd find out soon. Unable to say no, because William had been sending her the most exquisite paintings of the moorland flowers as each flowered in their turn, she'd agreed to meet him. The paintings always came with a little covering note to say he was very busy at the quarry but that he was thinking of her. And Hannah always sent a letter of thanks in return, saying she was thinking of him, too. Which was true; she was.

They weren't meeting out on the

moor, but in The Duchy Hotel in Princetown. The venue had been William's choice.

And now here she was, about to climb the steps to the hotel. William must have been watching from a window because he came rushing out to meet her.

'Hannah,' he said, taking both her hands in his, lifting them to his lips. 'It is so good to see you.'

'And I, you,' Hannah said.

William released her hands and, with a guiding hand under one elbow, ushered her into the hotel and through to a room which was full of tables covered in pristine cloths and pretty china. Almost all were occupied.

'A cream tea, I thought,' William said. 'Like the visitors.'

He guided her to a table that said *Reserved*, past people who were speaking in accents far different to her own. Or William's. Why, at one table they seemed to be speaking a foreign language.

'You guessed I'd come,' Hannah said, as William pulled out a chair for her to sit.

'I hoped with all my heart you would, and now you're here and looking so, well . . . the Scots have a word for it — *bonny*.'

'Am I?' Hannah said, her hands flying to her cheeks.

Is that what being with child was doing for her — making her look *bonny*?

'You are,' William said. 'And now that I have the running of the quarry on a more satisfactory footing, I will have more free time. So I hope to see more of you. You have the whole summer off school, Hannah. Will you let me show you parts of the moor that perhaps you've not seen yet? Would you like that?'

I'd like that very much, Hannah thought. But how obvious would her pregnancy be by the time the summer was over and school began again in September? And might William notice?

William was smiling at her, his eyes holding hers. He pushed his hair back off his forehead — a gesture Hannah found endearing, because so many of the little boys in school did the same thing.

'I can see you're giving it some thought.' William laughed nervously.

'I am,' Hannah said.

'Ah, here's the waitress with our tea,' William said.

Not just tea, Hannah saw. The waitress was pushing a trolley with a huge china teapot and a three-tiered cake stand, loaded high with not just scones, but cakes as well. Hannah felt her stomach rumble in anticipation. That was another thing about being with child — she seemed to be permanently hungry. Not that she was giving in to that hunger and eating more than she normally did. She'd hold off having to tell her ma, and everyone else, for as long as she could.

She *would* have to tell them all, and especially William. But not yet. For the moment she would enjoy the tea and cakes William was so kindly offering her.

8

Autumn 1903

The weather — torrential rain for the last two weeks in July, followed by hot days with frequent thunderstorms in the first week of August — had meant that William and Hannah had enjoyed fewer trips out in the pony and trap than William had planned.

But now, as August drew to a close, the weather was good again. William proposed a visit, with a picnic, to Spitchwick. And, it seemed, lots of visitors had planned the same thing. There was even a charabanc full of happy people out on some celebration or other with a crate of ale for the men. No need for a chaperone, Hannah smiled to herself, with all these people here! Not that her mother had even mentioned the word lately, caught up as she was in her own romance with

Edward Dyer and her job with the doctor.

'I have something for you,' William said, after they'd enjoyed pasties Hannah had made and some ginger beer William had brought, along with a slab of fruit cake the size of a house brick. It had been too delicious for words; Hannah had eaten two slices. 'For your birthday.'

'How do you know it's my birthday?'

'Ah,' William said. 'That would be telling.'

Hannah pleated her brow, thinking. William had been at school with Dr Tucker's brother and her own mother worked for Dr Tucker. It wouldn't have been so hard for William to find out when her birthday was, would it?

'I don't need anything — a present I mean — for my birthday,' Hannah said. 'The day out is lovely enough.'

'I'd still like you to have this,' William said gently. 'Hands out!'

A ripple of cold fear ran up Hannah's spine. The boys in school were always saying that to the girls, then they'd drop something like a dead mouse or a frog, or a huge, live spider in their open hands.

But Hannah did as she was told.

A locket. William was giving her a locket, placing it so carefully on her palms. An oval about the size of a pullet's egg on a fine gold chain. Hannah had never held anything so lovely in her hands before. The outside of the locket was engraved with a sprig of heather, and Hannah wondered if William had done the engraving himself.

'But I can't accept this,' Hannah said.

'Why not?'

'Because, it's well . . . well, it's the sort of thing . . . ' Hannah ran out of words.

'It's the sort of thing a man who cares deeply for a woman would give, Hannah,' William said. 'Here, let me show you. It opens.'

With a fingernail, William opened the

locket to reveal two miniature paintings. A picture of Hannah on one side, and a rocky outcrop of granite against an azure sky on the other.

Hannah's blood seemed to freeze in her veins. That rocky outcrop was the one Ralph had thrown her against when he . . .

'What's the matter, Hannah? Don't you like it?'

The painting of me, yes. But not the other one. How could she wear that around her neck? And how could she tell William why she couldn't?

William was looking concerned now.

'Something *is* wrong, Hannah, I know it is. Am I forcing myself on you . . . ?'

'No,' Hannah said. 'Never that.'

She shivered again at his choice of words. Ralph had *forced* himself on her.

She peered closely at her portrait in the locket. William had painted her with her hair over her shoulders, and at her throat he had painted the locket. In the painting she was smiling, gazing out adoringly. Was that how she looked at William? Could he see the love in her eyes? She looked up and saw he was looking at her with exactly the same look in *his* eyes.

Would that love still be there for her when he found out about the baby?

She ought not to have agreed to spend time with William. Her mind told her it was an unwise thing to have done, yet her heart had been telling her otherwise.

But it was her mind that was winning the contest now.

She closed the locket and wrapped her fingers around it, feeling the weight of it, the smoothness of the gold. Then she opened her hands. She lifted the locket by its chain.

'It's beautiful. And I appreciate your gesture in giving it to me. But I can't accept it.' She held it out towards William.

'It's Ralph, isn't it?' William's eyes darkened. He made a thin, taut line of his lips. 'You have stronger feelings for him than you do for me.'

Yes, it was Ralph, but not in the way William was suggesting.

'No, it's not like that. But something has happened. I've been trying to find the right moment to tell you . . . '

'Then tell me now.'

Hannah hadn't even told her mother yet. What if William were to say something in Huckstone House and Annie Leigh overheard and reported back? How disrespectful that would be.

'I can't. Not yet. I think it would be for the best if you take me home now, William. Please,' Hannah said.

★ ★ ★

On the 2nd September, the day before the new school term was to start, Hannah went to see Miss Pollyblank.

'I knew it was *something*, Miss French. I couldn't put my finger on what, but it's all becoming clear now.'

Hannah, her crossed hands resting on her stomach, sat straight-backed in the chair on the other side of Miss Pollyblank's fireplace.

'I'm sorry,' Hannah said, 'to let you and the children down.'

'I'm afraid you might find that it is yourself who has been let down. And I don't say that to chastise you. You aren't the first in this sort of situation and you certainly won't be the last. Does your mother know?'

'Not yet.'

Hannah was dreading that encounter.

'And the father of this child? You've told him?'

'No!' Hannah said, rather too forcefully because Miss Pollyblank jerked her head backwards as if in shock.

But she recovered quickly enough.

'And do I take it you are *not* going to tell him?'

Hannah shook her head.

'Very well, dear. That's your business. But, as you don't show yet, do you think you might work until, say, Christmas?'

Hannah's eyes widened of their own

volition. She hadn't been expecting *that* response. She'd been expecting to have her morals questioned and been told to leave the parish as soon as possible. But Christmas? Why, she'd be almost seven months by then. Everyone would notice.

'I don't think so. By my reckoning, the baby is due in February.'

'November then?' Miss Pollyblank said. 'With the colder weather, you could wear more clothes; looser clothes. I take it you've not been to see Dr Tucker, if your date is so vague?'

'Not yet,' Hannah said, blinking back tears. 'I haven't told anyone but you yet.'

'Ah. And now, seeing as your mother works for Dr Tucker, it's going to be difficult to go to see him, isn't it?'

'It is,' Hannah said. 'But today my mother's not working. Dr Tucker goes to the cottage hospital in Bovey Tracey on Thursdays. His pony and trap was in his drive when I passed by. I'm hoping to catch him before he goes.'

'Then we'll go together,' Miss Pollyblank said. 'I, too, once loved a man when perhaps I ought not to have done. And that's all I'm saying on the subject.'

Hannah gave herself a few moments to assimilate that last piece of rather surprising information and what Miss Pollyblank had meant by it.

Then she said, 'I'll see Dr Tucker on my own, and . . . '

'Nonsense,' Miss Pollyblank interrupted. 'Once you've had this baby and it's been adopted then I, for one, will be glad to have you back at the school and I shall tell the doctor that. I'm sure he'll know of somewhere you can go in your latter months.'

Hannah clasped her hands together and squeezed hard. Give the baby up for adoption?

Regardless of how it had been conceived, she'd never be able to do that, would she?

And she wasn't going to let Miss Pollyblank accompany her to the doctor either. But when she reached his house, Dr Tucker's pony and trap had gone.

★ ★ ★

William's mood was as miserable as the weather. A thick mist hovered over the moor, dulling sound. Even the constant banging of hammer on chisel in the quarry seemed to be muted.

He took off his coat and shook stone dust from it, before hanging it on the peg in the back hall. He wondered if Ralph was back yet. He'd been at the quarry for most of the day, much to William's surprise. He was hardly ever there these days, preferring to help the Hannafords up at Dewerbank while Matthew Hannaford was in hospital in Exeter.

At three o'clock Ralph had said he was calling it a day. William hadn't even looked up as he left.

But now, William noticed, Ralph's boots were placed on the mat ready for the maid to clean them. He was home somewhere.

William scooped a jug of water from the pail beside the kitchen sink and went up to his room to wash. It would be cold, but that would be just what he needed to clear his thoughts of Hannah.

The school term had started and he'd seen her shepherding children across the road from the school to the church for the beginning of term service. He'd gone over in his mind a million times as to why she had been unable to accept his gift. And why, on the journey back to Hillside Cottage, she'd said she thought it would be for the best if they didn't see one another. *For a while.* She'd added that after a few seconds hesitation.

I'll hang on to that — *for a while* — William thought. Her mother was seeing Edward Dyer; perhaps someone in her father's shoes wasn't going down well with Hannah, although he didn't think it could be that. Hannah wasn't one to begrudge anyone anything. No, Ralph had something to do with it, and the sooner he could get to the bottom of what it was, the better it would be.

'What the hell?'

William's bedroom door was wide open and Ralph was at the tallboy, rifling through William's things, his back to him, head bent in concentration.

He didn't even look round as William marched into the room.

'What the hell do you think you're doing in my room?' William demanded. He grabbed Ralph's shoulder and spun him round to face him.

Ralph had some of their mother's jewellery grasped in his closed fist.

'Taking my just share of Ma's jewellery, as you see,' Ralph said.

'It was left in trust to *me*, as well you know. Put it back.'

'Make me.'

'We're not in the playground now,' William said.

'Maybe not. But your thoughts are, I'll wager. One playground in particular, where Miss French holds court. Not seen you getting spruced up to meet her lately. Given you the brush off, has she?'

'Shut your mouth,' William said.

He wasn't going to discuss Hannah with anyone, and least of all with his brother.

'Looking for anything in particular?' William said coolly.

'Ma's engagement ring.'

'It's not there.'

'Where is it then?'

'Safety deposit box at the bank.'

'Then get it out. I'll make a deal with you. You get to keep all this,' Ralph dropped all the jewellery in his hand on top of the tallboy, 'and I'll have the engagement ring.'

'Over my dead body,' William said. 'You know as well as I do that a mother's jewellery is always passed to the eldest son for his wife. And so on down the line.'

Ralph shrugged. He knows he's beaten, William thought. Those were the rules and Ralph knew it.

'Not keeping it for Miss French, are you?' Ralph goaded. 'Because let me tell you, she's not as pure-as-the-driven-snow as you might think she is.'

'Meaning?' William said. He wasn't at all sure he wanted to hear what Ralph might be about to tell him.

'Wouldn't you like to know?' He scooped up the jewellery he'd dropped so carelessly just moments before. 'I'll take this instead. It should raise a fair amount; enough for what I want anyway.' And then, before William could stop him, Ralph ran for the door. 'Tell Uncle I won't be eating here tonight.'

And he was gone.

William put a hand in his trouser pocket, clasped his fingers around the locket he'd wanted Hannah to have. Thank God that hadn't been in the drawer. He still wanted her to have the locket, because in his heart he knew she loved him just as much as he loved her; it was there in her eyes when she looked at him.

* * *

Hannah couldn't get out of going to church on Sundays with her mother, although she'd tried. And now Edward Dyer, who seemed to have moved from his usual place in a pew at the back to the one Hannah and Edith sat in, had taken to joining them.

Today the church was packed for Harvest Festival, which was usually one of Hannah's favourite services. Most of the children from the school were there, excitedly clutching their offerings — a few apples here, a loaf of bread there. Jane Stokes was clutching a small basket filled to the brim with late blackberries. Hannah saw her look around to see if anyone was watching before taking one and popping it in her mouth.

Hannah smiled. She hoped her own

child *would* be a girl. Even a naughty one like Jane, who said words she shouldn't say and stole her harvest offerings.

'Well, well.' Edith leaned towards Hannah until they were shoulder to shoulder. 'Look who's just come in,' she whispered.

Hannah looked towards the aisle. The Hannafords. They hadn't been in church for weeks because Matthew Hannaford was ill, so rumour had it. Taken to the county hospital in Exeter for an operation of some sort.

Mrs Hannaford, with Miss Beth on her arm and Ralph Lawlor bringing up the rear, walked to the Hannaford pew at the front as though they'd paid not just for the pew but for the whole church.

It seemed that the Reverend Toop had been waiting for the Hannaford party to arrive, because he suddenly appeared from the vestry and the service began. Prayers were said for Matthew Hannaford, that he might be cured of his illness and back home soon.

And then came the first reading of the banns for the marriage of Miss Beth Hannaford to Mr Ralph Lawlor.

'Bit quick, if you get my meaning,' Edith whispered in Hannah's ear.

Hannah put a finger to her lips.

'Ssh.'

'Bun in the oven, I reckon,' Edith said, as the organ started up for the final hymn.

And she's not the only one, Hannah thought, except there won't be anyone adding my name to theirs in the reading of banns.

* * *

'Will you look at this?' Edith said.

'What?'

Hannah felt faint. She'd just felt the baby quicken for the first time. There was no denying her condition now.

Miss Pollyblank had loaned her a book on Mothercraft. Hannah had wondered where she'd come by it — and why — because it was quite old. She hadn't liked to ask, especially after her employer's unguarded remark that she, too, had loved a man, perhaps unwisely.

So far, it seemed, Hannah was having a textbook pregnancy. She had yet to go and see Dr Tucker though, having declined Miss Pollyblank's offer to go with her some weeks back.

She grabbed for the back of the kitchen chair.

'Hannah?' her mother said. 'You look . . . '

'I'm fine,' Hannah cut in. 'Honestly. I must have been standing too long chopping up these vegetables for pickle.'

'If you say so. Oh, Hannah, you're not going to believe this.'

Her mother thrust an invitation card at her.

Hannah was reluctant to take it — she knew what it was. Miss Pollyblank had received just such a card and it was on the mantelpiece in her office.

'The Hannafords have only gone and invited us to the church for the wedding. And afterwards there's to be cake and tea for the whole parish in the church hall. What do you make of that? Seeing as they sacked us both!' Edith French roared with laughter. ' Seems they want a good turnout their side of the church for this shotgun wedding, don't it? Go on, take it. It won't bite.'

Hannah took the proffered card.

Mr and Mrs Matthew Hannaford
of Dewerbank
Request your company at the marriage
of their daughter,Elizabeth,
to *Mr Ralph Lawlor of*
Huckstone House.
The Parish Church of St. Michael and
All Angels, Princetown.
2.30pm Saturday, 17th October, 1903
Refreshments will be served
in the church hall afterwards.

'We'll have to have new hats,' Edith said.

'I don't see why,' Hannah said. 'You've got a hat.'

'You'm greener 'n grass sometimes,' Edith said. 'A wedding always begets another one. And I, for one, intend to have a new hat. Just in case anyone, who shall remain nameless, should notice and . . .'

'Oh, for goodness sake, Ma,' Hannah said. 'You're acting like a girl over Edward Dyer. I thought you said he didn't have any money?'

'Money isn't everything, girl,' Edith said. 'Although you'll be all right for a parcel of it if Mr William . . .'

'You can forget all about me and William getting married,' Hannah snapped, 'if that was what you were about to say.'

Edith sucked her breath in through gritted teeth.

'I don't know what's got into you lately, my girl, but I'm not liking your sharp ways. Here,' Edith said, reaching for the sugar bowl and thrusting it towards Hannah.

The words 'pot' and 'calling' and 'kettle' and 'black' came to mind, but Hannah didn't voice them.

''Ere. Take a spoonful of that to sweeten yourself up. And before you even think of protesting, we are both going to go and see Miss Beth and Mr Ralph tie the knot. What would they think if we were the only parishioners who didn't?'

Hannah's heart seemed to sink to somewhere around her boots. William would be at the wedding. She wouldn't be able to avoid seeing him. Should she tell her mother about the baby before the wedding — or afterwards?

9

Hannah ducked as the saucepan Edith had grasped in her hand, ready to hold the cabbage, came hurtling towards her.

'Ma!' Hannah shouted. 'Stop! I'm going to leave this house right now if you throw another thing!'

Already she'd been whacked around the head with a damp tea-towel, and had had a potato, leftover from the day before, hit her fair and square in the chest.

'I've a good mind to make you leave anyway!' Edith screamed back at her.

'I would if I had anywhere to go.'

'Less of your cheek. Seems those Lawlor men are tarred with the same brush,' Edith said. All the rage seemed to have leached out of her now and she flopped down onto a kitchen chair. 'There's Mr Ralph being dragged up the aisle by the Hannafords to do the right thing by their daughter, and now Mr William has got you in the same condition. A man like him won't . . . '

'William isn't the father, Ma,' Hannah said, wishing with all her heart that he was.

'I don't believe you. All those times you were out on the moor with him. Watching him paint indeed!'

'That's all I *was* doing, Ma,' Hannah said. 'I know you find it hard to believe, but that's the truth.'

'Then whose is it?'

Edith let her eyes stray from Hannah's face, down over her chest, to her stomach.

'I'm not saying. Ever.'

Edith snorted with derision.

'Hah!'

Hannah breathed a sigh of relief that Edith didn't bring up the fact Hannah had gone to Tavistock, alone, with Ralph on an 'errand' for the school.

'As you see, I'm not showing much yet,' she said, 'although I've had to move the button on my skirt twice now.

Miss Pollyblank says . . . '

'You told *her* before you told *me*?'

'I had to. The realisation of my condition was making me snappy with the children.'

Not strictly true, but a good enough explanation.

Hannah waited for her mother — her hands propping up her head now, as though it was the weight of nations — to say something else; to ask questions perhaps. The silence in the room between them was palpable.

The nights were drawing in again now and Hannah lit the oil lamp. Still her mother didn't speak.

'I'll go on up to bed,' Hannah said. 'I'm not hungry.'

'Not before I've said what I'm going to say,' Edith said. 'Sit down.'

Hannah placed her hands, one on top of the other, on the table in front of her.

'You've spoiled everything,' Edith said.

'Not entirely on my own, Ma. It takes . . . '

'I don't mean *you*. I mean for *me*. With Edward. There's him a pillar of the church, with all his children married before they had their babies, and now there's you . . . '

'I'm not listening to this,' Hannah said. She stood up quickly, knocking her chair over. 'All you think of is yourself. It's all you've ever thought of. All those lies that you were ill on a Sunday and you weren't at all; you just wanted me out of the house so Mr Dyer could come a-courting. And do things you probably don't want me to know about.' Hannah halted, drew a breath, giving Edith chance to speak but she didn't. So Hannah carried on. 'You haven't bothered to ask me how I am. Or if I've seen Dr Tucker.'

'Oh, good Lord,' Edith said. 'I quite forgot he should know. That'll be my job gone and all, I expect.'

'Or when it's due,' Hannah said, ignoring her mother's second show of selfishness.

'It don't matter when. You won't be

here when you have it. My cousin, Maude, lives down Plymouth way and you can go and stop with her. When you've had it, you'll be giving it for *adoption* straight after.' Edith swivelled round in her chair to look Hannah in the face on the word 'adoption'.

'That,' Hannah said, as she hurried towards the stairs, 'is for me to decide.'

* * *

'It's going to reflect badly on us if you don't be my groomsman,' Ralph said.

'On *you*,' William said. 'You should have thought of that before selling all our mother's jewellery.'

'There wouldn't have been any need if only you'd given me her engagement ring. I couldn't give Beth a cheap, paste ring off the market, could I?'

'If you hadn't squandered your allowance on women and drink and God only knows what else, you would have been able to buy her a decent enough ring. And you didn't have to get her with child either. You don't imagine for one moment that the entire parish is going to believe the reason for the hasty match is because her father is ill and wants to see her wed before he dies.'

Ralph smirked.

'He's being sent home from hospital for the ceremony. Giving her away. And talking of the *entire* parish, I saw to it that Mrs French and her lovely daughter are invited. Mrs Hannaford wasn't keen to begin with, but I managed to persuade her it would look bad if they were the *only* parishioners not there.'

'Hannah . . . ' William began, but Ralph cut him short.

'There's only one Mrs French around here, and she has just the one daughter. Hannah. Pity you didn't act more like a red-blooded man and less like a gentleman around her, then we could have made it a double wedding.'

'And you think the Hannafords would want their daughter to share her wedding day with former servants? If you do, then your brain is well and truly addled.'

Yes, Ralph was right. He had behaved like a gentleman towards Hannah, but that didn't mean he hadn't had to suppress his red-bloodedness. Just seeing her made him want to kiss her until his lips ached. And his body yearned to make love to her, to hold her in his arms all through the night, so that when they woke in the morning, they could do it all over again.

'Sleep on it, Will,' Ralph said, all smiles now. 'I could ask Aaron Newsome to be my best man, but I'd rather it was you. And so would Uncle Charles. We must put up a united family front.'

'The answer,' William said, 'is still no.'

★　★　★

'Well, there's a turn-up for the books,' Edith said.

The church was a hubbub of noise, every pew filled. All they were waiting for now was the bridal party. Hannah knew exactly what her mother had meant by her remark. Ralph Lawlor was standing, his back to the congregation, by the lectern. On his right hand, as groomsman, was Aaron Newsome, landlord of The Plume of Feathers; Aaron Newsome, and not his brother, William, as everyone would be expecting.

Hannah sat up taller in her seat to peer over heads, between them, to see if she could spy William. Charles Lawlor was sitting in the front row, with Mrs Leigh on one side and a man Hannah didn't recognise on the other. Another servant perhaps.

But no William. Oh yes, there he was, sitting three rows back with some of the quarry workers and their wives. As though he had felt her looking at him, William turned, looked straight at her and smiled. As though there had been no bad feeling between them over the locket.

Edith saw the smile.

'And straight after this little shindig, we're going to put it about you're off to Plymouth to take care of Cousin Maude. Oh,' her voice softened and she checked her hat was on straight, although it had been checked a dozen times before leaving the house. 'Here's Edward.'

Edward Dyer slid along the pew towards Edith, placing his hand on hers.

Hannah had never felt so alone in her life.

⋆ ⋆ ⋆

The next morning, while her mother was still in bed, Hannah left the cottage, careful not to let the door bang as she went. First she went to the school and put a letter for Miss Pollyblank through the door. Then she hurried along the road to Dr Tucker's. He was always up early — the whole area knew it. He had always made a point of letting everyone know they could call on their way to work if they had any worries, and that they didn't have to wait for surgery hours which were often inconvenient for workers. If the lamp was lit in his porch, then anyone could knock. It was lit now.

'Hannah?' Dr Tucker said, opening the door wide. The smile on his face that he always had when greeting patients or callers, slipped to one of concern. 'Is it your mother? Is she not well?'

'My ma's fine, Doctor,' Hannah said. 'It's me. And I know it's a Sunday and I wouldn't normally disturb your day of rest, but I need to talk to you.'

'Of course.'

He ushered Hannah into his hallway, closing the door behind her.

'I'm sorry to be *this* early,' Hannah said. She saw that the clock in Dr Tucker's hallway wasn't showing 6.30 a.m. yet.

Dr Tucker spread his hands wide,

gesturing it was no problem.

He opened the door into his consulting room.

But before Hannah sat on the chair he indicated was for her, she blurted out why she had come. And that her mother had arranged for her to go to Plymouth until the baby was born. And that her mother was insisting she give the child up for adoption. How she'd written to Miss Pollyblank and put the letter through her door just moments ago.

'First things first, Hannah,' the doctor said. 'If you'll just hop up on the examination table, I'll take a look at you.'

He poured water from a jug into a bowl and washed his hands vigorously with a bar of green soap, while Hannah did as she was told.

The examination was soon over, although it made her tearful that the doctor was being so gentle, so kind, so understanding, when all she'd had from her own mother were angry words.

'My ma won't lose her job with you over this, will she, Doctor?'

'I don't see why she should. In fact, I wouldn't want to lose her. She's very thorough in her work.'

'Then can I write her a note? And will you give it to her?'

'I can. But ... oh, I see. You're running away because you don't want to go to Plymouth, is that it?'

'Maude is the last person I want around me. Her sour attitude would be bad for my unborn child. And for me.'

'Quite,' the doctor said. 'But where are you going?'

'I can get the train to Plymouth, and from there to Exeter perhaps. Or Bristol. Somewhere big where no-one will know me. I'm sure I'll be able to find lodgings. I have savings ... '

'Stop! You haven't thought this through. And I can understand why not. I have a better idea. How would you feel about going to stay with my brother, Simon, and his wife, until your time? They live at Huccaby House.

They have no servants,' Dr Tucker smiled at Hannah. So no-one to tell tales, the smile said. 'Simon is a liberal and doesn't like the class system. My sister-in-law is a little lame and would be glad of help. I can persuade my brother that help for his lame wife is not the same as having a servant. No-one would know you were there, I'm . . . '

'Oh, but they might,' Hannah interrupted.

William had been at university with Dr Tucker's brother. He'd told her he had.

'Who?'

Hannah put her hands over her mouth. She couldn't say 'William' could she? Or Dr Tucker would put two and two together and make a dozen of it, as her mother had, wouldn't he?

She was beginning to feel how she imagined a fly might feel caught up in a spider's web. Becoming increasingly tangled up and trapped with no escape.

Not knowing what to do or what to

say, she plunged her hands in the pockets of her coat and pulled out a handkerchief to blow her nose — not that it needed blowing, but it was something to do.

But to her horror, the letter she had written for William, which she'd been planning to post at the post office before catching the train, fell from her pocket onto the doctor's parquet floor. He picked it up.

'Ah,' he said. 'William Lawlor . . . '

'No, Doctor! William's not the father, if that's what you're thinking. I know I've been seen with him out on the moor and riding in the pony and trap, but it's not him.'

'But you're not going to tell either me or Mr William who the father is?'

'No.'

'It's your right not to, Hannah.'

Someone rang the doctor's door bell then and Hannah's heart skipped a beat. Whoever was there would see her going out and . . .

'You don't have to go, Hannah,' the

doctor said, interrupting her thoughts. 'I can take you through to the kitchen and my wife. And then, when I've seen the next patient, I can take you and whatever it is you have in that bag there to my brother at Huccaby House. I won't breathe a word to anyone — not even to your mother — that that's where you are. Although, of course, I will assure her you are safe and well. I can even, if you want me to, see that Mr William gets your letter.'

The doctor still had it in his hand.

'Thank you,' Hannah said. 'I'd like to take advantage of everything you've said.'

'18th October 1903
Dear, dear William,

I am so sad to be writing this letter to you, because I do care for you very much and I am going to miss seeing you, although we haven't seen much of one another of late, have we? I do hope you understand my reasons for refusing the beautiful locket you wanted me to have. I don't think your family would ever accept me as your wife — if that was your hope in offering it to me. I saw the way you smiled at me in the church yesterday and I think you have forgiven me — I hope so anyway.

But something has happened — something too terrible to put into words. I'm sorry I avoided you after the wedding of your brother and Miss Beth, and that I didn't attend the tea afterwards in the church hall. But I didn't feel well.

My mother's cousin, Maude, is ill and I'm to go to Plymouth to care for her. In fact, by the time you are reading this, I will be there. It means, of course, that I have resigned my position at the school. I don't know when I will be back. Certainly it won't be for Christmas.

I hope all goes well for you at the quarry. And with your painting. I shall always treasure the painting *you sent me of us dancing on the grass.*

Yours, with fond affection,
Hannah.'

William read Hannah's letter for at least the sixth time and he still didn't believe a word of it.

Her mother's cousin ill in Plymouth indeed. He had a gut feeling that Ralph had something to do with this, and William intended to get to the bottom of it. Just as soon as Ralph and his new wife were back from their honeymoon.

But first he would go and see Mrs French.

★   ★   ★

Hannah couldn't have been more surprised at the welcome Dr Tucker's brother and his wife gave her. Mr Tucker's wife insisted that Hannah call her by her Christian name, Martha. She showed Hannah to a room on the second floor of the three storey house.

'It will be warmer here than up in the attic. And the windows are larger here, so you can sit and look at the view if you become tired.'

'It's wonderful,' Hannah said, her mind in a daze that this was all happening so fast. 'I'm so grateful . . . '

Then, as though mentioning the word 'tired' had made her so, Hannah yawned, covering her mouth with her hands in embarrassment at her rudeness.

Martha merely laughed.

'My lame leg has the same effect sometimes. Simon understands, though, if I yawn at inappropriate times.'

Martha chuckled at what she knew those inappropriate times to be, but about which Hannah could only make a wild guess — and that guess was, in the loving times with Simon.

And then, as though reading Hannah's mind, Martha said, 'Simon and I can't have children. It isn't only my leg that is lame. But enough of that. I'll leave you to unpack and to have a little rest if you need one after all the emotion of this morning. Lunch will be a little later today — one o'clock.'

And then Martha hobbled away awkwardly and Hannah's heart lurched for her.

But then a thought came, unbidden, into her head. Had Dr Tucker suggested she come here, so that when her baby was born she hand it over to Simon and Martha?

* * *

'It's no good you keeping on asking, Mr William,' Mrs French said. She was twisting her hands over and over in front of her. 'I can't give you my cousin's address. It wouldn't be right. You can't just go calling . . . '

'Will you tell me the real reason Hannah has gone to Plymouth — if that, indeed, is where she is?'

William saw Mrs French's colour rise then.

'I wasn't expecting her to be gone so

soon, Mr William, and that's the truth. Her wrote me a letter, though.' Mrs French pointed to an envelope on the table, the flap open, and a sheet of paper half in and half out of it.

Mrs French took a handkerchief from her apron pocket and blew her nose. Her eyes were welling with tears.

'An' 'er ain't in Plymouth neither. 'Er said 'er'd rather die than go to that stagnant place where her soul would be sucked dry. Oh, Mr William, I don't know what to do. I shouldn't have been so 'ard on 'er — thinking only of meself.'

William was alarmed now.

'And you have no idea where she is?'

'I don't, no. But the doctor do, and he won't tell. All he said were that she was safe and would be well cared for . . .'

'Thank you, Mrs French,' William said. 'That's all I need to know!'

And then he ran from the cottage, unloosed his horse from its tether, and leapt into the saddle.

'Go, Samson! Go!'

10

'And you can assure me Hannah isn't wasting away with some dreaded illness? Consumption perhaps?'

The doctor laughed.

'You can be assured it's nothing so serious.'

William heaved a sigh of relief.

'If you won't tell me what exactly is wrong with her, or where she is, Doctor,' he said, 'then will you see she gets my letter? When I've written one, that is.'

Dr Tucker studied William as though he were a disease, William thought, although the only disease he had was lovesickness, if that could be termed an illness.

'I will,' the doctor said. 'But what I can't promise is that she will reply.'

'That will be for Hannah to decide,' William said. 'But at least when she gets my letter, she'll know I care about her.'

'Then write it,' the doctor said. 'Bring it here, and any others you care to write, and I'll see she gets it.' And the doctor smiled at William, shook his hand heartily. 'And if that is all I can help you with . . . '

'It is,' William said. 'Thank you.'

He couldn't wait to get home and write to Hannah.

* * *

William's letters came thick and fast, always brought by hand by Dr Tucker or his wife. Sometimes the envelope would contain a drawing or a small painting of moorland flowers and butterflies, and a short note. *'One more for your collection, Hannah.'* And sometimes the letters were longer, spilling out all his hopes and dreams for the future; he was just months away now from getting a quarry manager in, seeing as Ralph was living at Dewerbank with his wife and her parents. He hoped, he said, that one day he and Hannah would be reunited. Hannah treasured every single letter.

And she replied to every single one, too, although in a rather more guarded way. Neither she, nor William, mentioned Plymouth or the sick relative Hannah was supposed to be nursing.

As well as letters, William sent gifts: scented soap and a pair of fur-lined gloves. A pen and some ink. And books. Two books of poetry, and books on all the places William said he would like to visit one day to paint — Italy and France. And one book that surprised Hannah more than the others; a book on Art Nouveau. What would Miss Pollyblank think if she were to suggest they decorate the walls of the school Art Nouveau fashion? Not that Hannah would be returning to the school now.

'I don't know why you don't just marry him?' Martha laughed, as Hannah handed her yet another letter to be taken to Dr Tucker to be passed on.

The postman would have taken it when he delivered letters to Huccaby House, but Hannah and Martha had decided between them that that wouldn't be a good idea. Fred Adams would almost certainly mention to someone that he was taking letters on a regular basis from Huccaby House to William Lawlor. And that would never do.

'Because he hasn't asked me,' Hannah said. Not in so many words, she thought but didn't add, although he seemed to be including her more and more in his dreams and plans with each letter.

She had settled in well with Simon and Martha Tucker. They were both kindness itself. To 'earn' her keep, Hannah made curtains and other household items from material Martha bought at market. She always came back with a length of material — *'I was practically given it, Hannah, it was so reasonable'* — for Hannah to make clothes for herself that would fit her ever-expanding body. And always there would be some cotton lawn or some winceyette for Hannah to make vests and other little garments for her unborn baby.

Under cover of darkness, Hannah walked the sheep tracks out onto the moor — sometimes with Simon, but mostly on her own — to get exercise.

At Christmas they made up a parcel of food and presents for Hannah's mother, delivered to Dr Tucker for him to pass on so she wouldn't suspect where Hannah was.

And in return, much to Hannah's surprise, she received a layette; the tiniest pair of leggings and jacket with a bonnet to match, in the palest of pale lemon wool. Edith was no knitter but she'd obviously laboured over this. Had she told Edward Dyer about her condition? Hannah wondered. Was Edith still seeing him? Or was the shame of having a daughter with child, and out of wedlock, too much to bear?

There had been a Christmas card in with her mother's parcel, wishing Hannah the compliments of the season. Nothing more.

William sent her the locket. And in his note he told her that if she returned it, then he would only send it back again. So Hannah had fastened it around her neck and she was never without it now.

'Not long now,' Hannah said, patting her bump.

The baby was more active by the day. Dr Tucker was calling to see her — and his brother and sister-in-law, of course — more frequently now that January was nearly over. So far, no-one at all had suggested that Hannah hand her baby to Simon and Martha when it was born. And thank goodness for that, because Hannah knew now she'd never be able to.

'Looks like snow,' Martha said.

Hannah raced to the window. One of her biggest fears these days was going into labour in a snowstorm. Princetown was often cut off from the outside world entirely in winter, and even the train was unable to make the journey down to Plymouth.

★ ★ ★

And then, on the 2nd February, Hannah opened one of William's letters to read the words she had been dreading.

> *'Dearest Hannah,*
> *I am writing to say you will not be hearing from me for a while. I do not . . . '*

Hannah's eyes swam with tears as she read on.

'Oh,' she said out loud. 'Charles Lawlor has died suddenly and peacefully in his sleep.'

And William was only letting her know he would have much to do with the administration of his uncle's estate.

He would have to go to London to sign business documents and he had no idea how long it would take.

Hannah read on.

' . . . and as the quarry is now on a firmer footing financially, I will soon be in a position to engage a manager. And then I can begin to think of fulfilling my dreams to travel.'

Hannah scrunched William's letter up into a ball.

'And those plans more than likely won't include a baby amongst the luggage. Your brother's baby.'

She hurled the letter towards the wastepaper basket in the corner of the room.

And that was when she felt the first twinge of labour.

* * *

'A girl. Hannah, you have a daughter.'

Hannah, her eyes still screwed tight with the concentration — and not inconsiderable pain — of giving birth, was reluctant to open them.

'Has she got everything she should have?' Hannah asked. 'Ten fingers? Ten toes?'

Dr Tucker laughed.

'She has. And she's got the biggest mop of black hair I've ever seen on a newborn. If only you'd open your eyes, you'd see what a beautiful daughter you have.'

'Black hair?'

'Most newborns do have black hair, Hannah. Often it changes. But I don't think this little one is likely to turn out to be fair-haired.'

Ralph. Her baby was just like Ralph, wasn't she? Would she love her as much as she ought to? The baby hadn't asked to be born, had she?

Slowly, Hannah opened her eyes.

'Take her,' Martha said, her sleeves rolled up past her elbows and the baby cradled in her arms. 'She's beautiful. Really beautiful. So perfect.'

Hannah had been glad of Martha's hand to hold as each contraction came and threatened to overwhelm her. And she'd been happy for Martha when Dr Tucker had handed her the baby while he dealt with other things Hannah didn't want to think about. How undignified giving birth was. But now she could hear the tears in Martha's voice that she was never going to have a beautiful, perfect baby of her own.

Hannah stretched out her arms and Martha placed the baby — pink and plump and bawling, and with blood on her head and one shoulder — in them.

'One quick cuddle, Hannah,' Dr Tucker said, 'and then I'll weigh her. Wash her. And she'll need swaddling, so she doesn't catch cold.'

And then? Hannah thought. What then? She wouldn't be able to stay with Simon and Martha forever. Not now. She'd heard the longing in Martha's voice and it wouldn't be fair on the woman.

'Could someone tell my mother?' Hannah asked.

Dr Tucker said that he would, just as

soon as he could. A look had passed between the doctor and his sister-in-law as he spoke, but Hannah was too exhausted from the birth to give much thought to what that look conveyed.

She kissed the top of her daughter's head. Surely her mother would fall in love with her granddaughter, wouldn't she?

★　★　★

Letters. Hannah was sick of getting letters. It was as though she had leprosy or some other thing that meant she had to be in quarantine. She'd heard nothing from William in over two weeks now, although that was to be expected. But letters weren't the same as seeing William, watching him paint, hearing him hum some tune as he worked, looking up at her from time to time and smiling at her in surprise and delight as though he'd forgotten for a moment she was there, but pleased to see she was. The summer when they'd got to know one another, come to love one another, seemed so long ago now.

Did he know she'd had a child? And if he did, was that why he was distancing himself from her?

And now another letter — but not from William. Her name had been written on the outside of the envelope in her mother's ill-formed handwriting this time. Hannah ripped it open. How had it taken her mother two weeks to write, when Dr Tucker had told her the same day that she had a granddaughter? Or had he?

Quickly Hannah read the very short note.

Married. Edith had married Edward Dyer on New Year's Day at the Registry Office in Plymouth and had moved into his cottage. She hadn't told Edward about Hannah's baby, and she hoped Hannah had done the sensible thing and given it up for adoption so he would never know. She had returned the tenancy agreement of Hillside Cottage to the Duchy. She was no longer working for Dr Tucker. She hoped — Edith had written — that the baby had gone to parents who would give her a better life than Hannah could. And she also hoped that Hannah would dress her in the things she had knitted for her — '*something decent, at least*' had been her actual words.

Hannah returned her mother's letter to the envelope. She felt neither anger nor sadness, just a cold detachment that chilled her. How could her mother not have felt the rush of love for *her*, as Hannah felt for her own child, regardless of the circumstances of her conception?

The baby was asleep still, so Hannah picked up her sewing; she was making a blouse for Martha, having surprised herself by how much she enjoyed working with a needle and thread and that she had an aptitude for it. She was able to adapt patterns to disguise Martha's twisted body and the slight hump of her right shoulder.

But the baby stirred. Hannah had yet

to give her a name. And to register her — although there was plenty of time yet for doing that. Simon had said he would ask the Reverend Toop to come to the house to christen the baby if that was what Hannah would prefer.

Hannah put down the sewing and picked up her daughter from the cradle.

'Hope,' she said. 'I'm going to call you Hope. With no home to go back to, that's all we both have now.'

* * *

'This pantomime has gone on long enough, Doctor,' William said. 'I have to see Hannah, don't you understand?'

He'd refused the doctor's offer to sit, preferring to stand — arms folded — fair and square in front of Dr Tucker until he got some answers.

'I'm sure the frustration of not knowing . . . '

'I'm more than grateful to you for being the go-between for our letters. But I'll ask you one question, Doctor.

Have you not known the burning intensity, the aching longing of loving someone, and not being able to see that person, touch them, smell their special scent? See your love for that person reflected back to you in their eyes?'

'Rather more than one question there,' the doctor said, but William was relieved to see he was smiling. Yes, the good doctor had known all that.

'So you *have*. I can see it in your face.'

'Then you missed your vocation if you can read your 'patient' so well, William. But I'll ask *you* a question. Why are you so very desperate at this moment, when for months now it's seemed as though you had settled quite happily into the giving and receiving of letters between you and Hannah?'

'I had no other option. But my circumstances have changed. As you know, my uncle has died. I've appointed a manager to run the quarry. My brother is barely speaking to me. I don't know that I want to stay here any longer. And yet, because of Hannah, I can't go. I'd like her to come with me, and I need to see her, to ask her . . . '

'Stop!' Dr Tucker put up a hand. 'Sit.' He reached for William's arm and William allowed himself to be led to the chair and gently eased into it.

Oh God, the doctor was going to tell him Hannah was dead or dying and that someone else had been writing her letters, wasn't he?

'William,' the doctor said. 'I am breaking every oath I ever made as a doctor in telling you this. Hannah is staying with Simon and Martha. She has had a child.'

'Martha?'

'No. Hannah. A daughter. And a quite, quite beautiful one at that. She has a mop of thick, black hair. Eyes that are blue now but which, I'm sure, will change to the deepest brown. She's a large baby — longer legs and arms than most newborns. I know she's not your child, but . . . '

'She's my brother's child, isn't she?'
William said.

'Hannah hasn't said as much, although I've been in this profession long enough to know Hannah was hiding some unsavoury fact from me. I didn't press her. I'm a doctor not a judge.'

'And a benevolent one,' William said. 'You gave Hannah's mother a job when I asked for your help.'

'Edith French no longer works for me. She married Edward Dyer in the New Year. And she's recently given up the tenancy on Hillside Cottage. To my knowledge, Edith French has neither seen her granddaughter, nor wants to. Hannah and her child won't be able to stop with Simon and Martha forever. Are you understanding why I am telling you all this?'

Hannah was homeless now, wasn't she? And with a mother who quite obviously didn't care for her own daughter or want to see her grand-daughter.

'Every single nuance,' William said. 'I'd better not waste another single moment getting to Huccaby House, had I?'

*   *   *

'And that's the truth,' Hannah said.

Although what she'd had to tell William had obviously pained him to hear, the overriding feeling Hannah had was joy that William was with her at last. In person, and not just a name on the end of a letter. She'd hardly dared believe it when Martha had said Hannah had a caller — a gentleman caller — and that she'd made the breakfast room available to them both for as long as they needed. Martha, in the meantime, would look after Hope.

Hannah placed her palms together, prayer fashion, and slid them into the folds of her dress between her knees to stop herself from throwing her arms around William's neck. He'd arrived to see her, his bag bulging with presents

219

for the baby: a silver teething ring, a gold bracelet, a book of nursery rhymes with beautifully painted colour plates. Things, William said, that had been his own and which he hoped Hannah would accept, because he'd not had the time to go and buy new things.

'You could take out a prosecution against him,' William said, his face stony. 'He's an animal. I'm sure . . . '

'No!' Hannah said. 'Never that. I wouldn't want to have to face your brother in a court of law, and I wouldn't want the Lawlor name — your name, too — in the newspapers next to mine in such circumstances.'

'I have to ask,' William said. 'Does Ralph know about Hope?'

'No. And I'm not going to tell him.'

'Can I see her?'

'Hope?'

'Of *course*, Hope. Who else did you think I meant?'

'I'll fetch her,' Hannah said, rising to her feet. She thought her legs might be in danger of not holding her up, she was so excited and anxious and relieved in equal measure that William had asked to see her child.

When Hannah returned with Hope in her arms, William had a sketchpad out, and a pencil.

'I thought I'd draw her. And you. Do you mind?'

'I'd love you to,' Hannah said.

For now William was with her and what the future held she didn't know. But then, how do any of us know what the future holds? If William wasn't to be part of her future, then she was sure he would give her his drawing of her and Hope, and at least she would have that.

Hannah sat with the sleeping Hope in her arms. And while she sat, William sketched. And talked. How his uncle had left him considerable means, as well as a half share in the quarry. How he had a manager in at Furzevale now and he was in the process of letting Huckstone House to tenants — Londoners who wanted it for use in the summer months. How Italy and

France, and possibly Spain, were calling with an urgency he was finding hard to resist.

'Then don't,' Hannah said. 'You'll only regret it if you don't go. You can write to me and tell . . . '

'I could do better than that,' William said. 'You can come with me and see it all for yourself. If you'd like to.'

Just me? Hannah thought. Did William think she was going to leave the baby with Simon and Martha? Give her up for adoption, as so many in her situation were forced to do?

On impulse, Hannah dropped a kiss on her sleeping daughter's head.

'And Hope, of course,' William said, his voice thick with emotion. 'We can't leave her behind, can we? Hope is a Lawlor, and so am I. I promise I will be the best father to her I know how. I thought Italy first. It will be warmer there for a baby, especially in the south. Sicily perhaps? There's an excellent rail network, so I'm told.'

Anywhere, Hannah wanted to say, as

long as it's with you, but the words wouldn't come. William's words were wrapping themselves around her heart, squeezing tight, making her feel more loved than she'd ever dreamed she would be.

'Hannah?' William said.

He put his sketchpad and pencil on a side table. Then he rose from his seat and came to kneel on the rug beside Hannah and Hope.

He placed his hands on either side of Hannah's face and kissed her lips. Just a light kiss at first, much as the kiss she'd just given Hope, but then his lips found hers again and this time the kiss lingered, warming her, thrilling her. Full of promise.

'Do say you'll come,' William said. 'Both of you.'

'I have so little to pack,' Hannah said, smiling at him. 'It shouldn't take me long. Now, I wonder if Simon and Martha might have a case I could have . . . '

We do hope that you have enjoyed reading this large print book.

Did you know that all of our titles are available for purchase?

We publish a wide range of high quality large print books including:
Romances, Mysteries, Classics
General Fiction
Non Fiction and Westerns

Special interest titles available in large print are:
The Little Oxford Dictionary
Music Book, Song Book
Hymn Book, Service Book

Also available from us courtesy of Oxford University Press:
Young Readers' Dictionary
(large print edition)
Young Readers' Thesaurus
(large print edition)

For further information or a free brochure, please contact us at:
Ulverscroft Large Print Books Ltd.,
The Green, Bradgate Road, Anstey,
Leicester, LE7 7FU, England.
Tel: (00 44) **0116 236 4325**
Fax: (00 44) **0116 234 0205**